Graeme Smith is an accomplished exponent of Kenpo karate and is a Fourth Degree Black Belt.
He is fascinated by the Bronze Age and has found many artefacts from this period whilst metal detecting.
His other interests include collecting knapped flints, dog walking and meditation.
He currently works for the NHS.

This book is dedicated to my three wonderful children Todd, Jake and Lauren.
It is also dedicated to the memory of my parents Freddie and Trena Smith.

Graeme Richard Smith

THE AWAKENING OF ABRAHAM BROWN

AUSTIN MACAULEY
PUBLISHERS LTD.

A CIP catalogue record for this title is available from the British Library.

ISBN 978 1 84963 833 3

www.austinmacauley.com

First Published (2014)
Austin Macauley Publishers Ltd.
25 Canada Square
Canary Wharf
London
E14 5LB

Printed and bound in Great Britain

Acknowledgments

Grateful thanks to Ruth for the many hours of typing from the original handwritten manuscript.
My thanks to Dave King for our in depth and thought provoking conversations on life and the esoteric.

Chapter One

Southern France, August 1944

As he lay there, the bayonet plunged deep into his left shoulder piercing his dark skin, cutting through the flesh and then striking the scapula.

The German smiled as he twisted his rifle around, intensifying the pain and discomfort so much so that Abraham Brown was at the threshold between consciousness and unconsciousness. Abraham looked up and released a deep sigh – his whole being relaxed – mind, body, and soul, and deep within his psyche, all the pain that he had suffered in life together with his father, grandfather and all his ancestry since being taken from Africa as slaves two centuries before; all this pain, struggle, strife, everything, it all just melted away.

In his mind's eye he could see the truth, the truth that everyone looks for in life but rarely finds. His whole body was limp and he just lay there and looked up deep into the German's eyes. The German was called Hans Gruman; his two sons and wife had been killed in an Allied bombing raid two years before. He was full of hate – hatred of the English, Americans and Allies. He had been a good man at heart but life and the war had eaten away at that goodness and turned him slowly into a monster.

Abraham Brown lay there in pain, watched by the other five Germans and his two fellow American comrades. Hans pulled the bayonet out of Abraham Brown who now felt no pain and prayed silently in his heart. Hans raised the rifle high above Abraham's chest directly above the heart and uttered the words in German, "Die, black dog, die." Just as he intended to thrust the rifle's bayonet deep into Abraham' s chest and heart, their eyes met again, but this time in just a microsecond of time Hans saw the monster he had become. All the hate and blood lust was reflected back by Abraham's soul-searching brown eyes. Hans let out a scream and dropped the rifle. He staggered over to a raised clump of soil and grass, looked up into the heavens and slowly unholstered and drew out his side arm Luger. The other Germans had no idea of the horror Hans had seen when his eyes had met Abraham's and now they thought he was play acting some sort of game before killing the three American servicemen. Hans stood there looking to the heavens, his once smart uniform dishevelled and war torn. His face, hair and hands were dirty.

It was just past seven o'clock on the evening of a bright sunny day, Hans raised the gun to his head, the barrel against his right temple. There was a deadly silence all round until *bang* – Hans Gruman ended his life and slumped instantly to the ground. His fellow countrymen rushed over, not knowing what to do or what had just happened.

Earlier that day the men had all fought against each other after meeting on the edge of a wood on farmland in the south of France. The Americans had lost three comrades and the Germans two during the gun fight. Abraham and the others had surrendered when all their ammo was gone. They were tired and hungry and were making their way towards what they thought was Allied held territory when the Germans spotted them from a nearby lookout post and ambushed them.

Abraham sat up looking at the Germans in confusion over Hans's suicide. His two comrades, Patch Hancock and Indigo Templeton, sat close by expecting execution at any time, their hands tied behind their backs and their minds full of fear and desperation, unlike Abraham who had gone beyond such emotions and dread. Abraham sat holding his injury with his right hand; it didn't hurt that much anymore, it just ached. He looked at the Germans who were standing by Hans's body, then his eyes were drawn back to where he sat, for the rifle with attached bayonet lay just yards in front of him on the ground. Abraham, apart from his injuries, was a very fit young man of twenty-five and had been involved with athletics whilst at school. He still possessed speed and agility and knew that this was a chance not be missed, so in the blink of an eye he leapt forward, reaching for the rifle, and in no time at all was crouched in a kneeling position, the rifle now pointing towards the Germans.

"Let them have it!" shouted Patch Hancock. "Go on, shoot the bastards!"

But Abraham shouted to the Germans to sit, and dipped the end of the rifle up and down to show them. They all sat down, their faces full of hopelessness as they knew the war for them was ending and that the Allies would be victorious. They were once proud patriotic men but now after so much fighting and the death of many fellow Germans, there was little fight left in them. The terrible war had taken its toll on these men so they just sat looking down at the ground, the ground that they had once invaded in the name of the Fuhrer and Fatherland. The ground that so much blood had been spilt upon. French, German and Allied forces, men, women and children, animals and nature. Much of the beautiful countryside now scarred and grotesque. What a tragedy for humanity to experience, so much pain and suffering, so much humiliation and hatred.

Abraham shouted over to Patch and Indigo who were sitting together with their hands tied, "Quick," he said, "one of you get yourself over here and run your wrists along the bayonet to release your hands."

Patch Hancock immediately shuffled over to Abraham who held the rifle in the direction of the Germans and was cautious not to give them a chance to make a run for it or be in a position to retaliate. Patch reached Abraham and knelt to the side and in front of Abraham, sliding the rope that bound his hands along the bayonet edge. Soon his wrists were free and without hesitation he removed the bayonet from the rifle and went over to Indigo Templeton to release his hands.

"One of you take this rifle," said Abraham, who was now in some discomfort after holding the rifle for some time. Patch gave Indigo the bayonet and relieved Abraham of the rifle.

"Come with me," said Patch. He and Indigo approached the Germans to relieve them of any weapons they had. "Up, up!" shouted Patch to the enemy soldiers. "You search them Templeton, and throw any weapons over there."

"Show them no pity," added Patch, who really wanted any excuse to hurt them.

"Calm down," replied Indigo as he searched the five enemy soldiers.

Abraham watched and noticed that the light was fading, so he yelled over to the two of them, "Get them searched, tie them up and settled for the night."

Soon the five Germans were sitting, their wrists and ankles bound.

Abraham, Patch and Indigo took over the Germans' camp fire and went through everything that was lying around, looking for food mainly and taking the German weapons for themselves as they had no ammo for their own.

The three men sat by the fire eating and drinking. Abraham Brown had a linen makeshift bandage taped over the wound to his shoulder.

"What's the plan then?" said Indigo to Abraham and Patch.

"Well," said the other two between them, "we had better see if we can get any information from the krauts as to where we are and what they are doing here next to this wood."

"OK," replied Indigo whilst scratching his unshaven chin.

"And let's gag them overnight to stop them scheming up any monkey business," said Patch.

The three men walked over to where the Germans sat. "*Sprechen sie Englisch*," said Indigo to the five of them.

They shook their heads from side to side, one of them saying, "*Nien*." The German soldiers were then gagged and left for the night; they were twenty-five feet away and easy to keep an eye on, but not too close to suddenly try something and take Abraham and the others by surprise.

"What about the dead one who topped himself?" said Indigo.

"We'll let the others bury him in the morning," replied Patch.

Abraham felt tired, and as the three men chatted he soon fell into a deep, deep sleep.

"Shall we take it in turns to watch the krauts?" said Indigo.

"No, don't bother." replied Patch. "They're all bound and gagged and look as done in as us. They're not a real threat. Just keep that gun handy and if you hear a peep from the Germans, fire a shot in their direction."

As the fire faded and the flickering shadows merged into the darkness the three comrades slept, each of them dreaming under the night sky. The glow of the moon shone faintly behind the thin layer of cloud that glided softly by above them. Now it was time to dream, and just for a few hours escape the horror and nightmare that was war.

The air was warm and the night was quiet, with occasional gunfire in the distance, too far away to concern anyone.

As the soldiers slept they were being watched by a figure hiding nearby in some bushes.

Chapter Two

Abraham Brown was of Afro-American descent. He had been the victim of, and witnessed, racism upon himself and others during his lifetime, but nothing had compared to being tortured by a Nazi standing over him thrusting a bayonet vertically through his body, and then twisting it to inflict more pain and torture. "What sort of people are these Nazis?" he had thought to himself.

Abraham was five feet eleven inches tall, of average build. He had a round jolly face and was a fairly quiet man. He lived and worked on a small farm in Kentucky, a farm that his father ran until he was killed one day after falling from a grain silo. Abraham was fifteen when this happened and he had to take over his father's duties to provide for the family. In his heart he had secretly desired to find his way in the world and escape the poverty he lived in and was born into, but he loved his family so much that running the farm was a noble and worthwhile thing to do with his life, providing for his mother, sister and brother. He loved animals and nature and just wanted to get through the war in peace and return home as soon as possible. He knew, like most people, that killing was wrong, but had to go to war as did millions of others to stop the Nazis' cruel regime being inflicted upon mankind. He felt justified in being in a foreign land defending and liberating France and anywhere else from them.

As he slept, Abraham dreamt of a woman and two boys either side of her holding her hands. They were calling to someone in the distance. That person came to them and they all embraced, a warm glow of happiness flowed over them and Abraham. The person turned, and in his dream Abraham saw it was Hans Gruman. He did not know about Hans's family being killed in a bombing raid, so was it just a dream, a premonition, was Hans showing Abraham he was now at peace?

Something amazing, something magical, happened to Abraham that day – something deep inside, something that cannot be named but only felt. It was as if there had been a combination lock of infinite numbers, holding behind it the secrets of the universe, and that day whilst he lay there expecting to die, all the numbers lined up and opened the secret to life and living. The cosmos had unlocked its timeless secrets to him.

* * * * * * * * *

Indigo Templeton was a slim, handsome man. He had olive coloured skin; his mother had emigrated to America from Italy in 1920. He had blue eyes and a thin face, a pointed nose and a pencil moustache above his top lip, the sort that Errol Flynn or David Niven wore. His father was a doctor who had left England to settle in America in 1913. He was an only child and had many gambling debts back home in America. He had been named Indigo as both his parents' favourite colour was blue, and the day he was born the sky was clear and seemed to be more indigo than normal blue.

* * * * * * * * *

Patch Hancock was half Irish on his mother's side. He was quite a short, stocky man with curly ginger hair. He was usually unshaven with a half cigar in his mouth. His skin was pitted and he had a snub nose. His father was a drunk who had shown no affection to Patch when he was a child and he eventually died of cirrhosis of the liver when Patch was twelve years old. Patch's real name was Scott, and he had a large birthmark on the left-hand side of his face and surrounding his eye. It was a large area of brown coloured skin which looked like a patch that a dog may have had, so his father never called him anything other than Patch. Over the years everyone called him the same, a fact that he really loathed and hated but accepted as he was stuck with the birthmark for life.

* * * * * * * *

"Come on you two, wake up!" said Patch in a disgruntled voice.

"What time is it?" said Indigo. "And was yesterday a bad dream or are we really stuck in this shithole place with five krauts to babysit?"

"Well, I ain't babysitting no krauts for sure," replied Patch. "They can stay here and rot for all I care."

Abraham sat up and looked at the other two. "Let's just get our stuff, have some food and get the hell out of here," he said. "We can untie the Germans and leave them. How can they hurt us with no weapons? They must be hungry as well. They can go that way and we can go eastward."

The fire from the previous evening was now just smouldering ash so Indigo said to Abraham and Patch, "I'm going into that wood to get some fallen branches and anything else that might burn. I'll give the krauts a kick on the way to wake them up." Indigo walked over to where the five Germans sat slumped. "Holy shit!" he yelled as he looked down at them to discover that all five had had their throats cut. Abraham and Patch ran over

"What the fuck!" exclaimed Patch. The three men stood in disbelief, each in turn declaring they had nothing to do with it and asking themselves which of the others had done it. "One of us must have done it," stated Patch.

"Not me," said both Indigo and Abraham in unison. The three men stood there for what seemed ages; they looked down at the slain German soldiers and then at each other in a suspicious manner.

Indigo eventually knelt down to examine the bodies. As he did so he looked up and asked, "Either of you two left-handed?"

"No, why?" came the same reply from both men.

Indigo explained what he had discovered. "Well whoever did this drew the blade from right to left, that is from their far side and towards them, so I guess they should be left-handed maybe?"

"That proves nothing," said Patch who went on to say, "I don't care who killed them but it wasn't me. They are the enemy and this is a gawd damn war we are in, not a picnic, so let's just get the hell out of this place and move on."

Indigo replied, "Let's just have a look around first to see if there is anything that can shed a clue as to what this is all about."

The three men spread out in different directions.

Abraham looked around at the edge of the wood and started to feel uneasy. He came to an opening which had many footprints leading to and from it. He decided to venture in and investigate. Just inside the wood stood an old shack, timeworn and in disrepair. Abraham approached and walked around the shack; many footprints lay in the moist woodland soil. When he had circled the shack, which had no windows and smelt of damp decaying wood, he noticed that a new padlock had been attached to the door. "That's odd," he thought to himself and called out to the others to come to him. As Abraham waited for them he began to feel uneasy about the shack, and as he looked he noticed a dark aura around it. He thought it was just the light being dimmed by the trees or some shadow effect upon it, but what he was seeing was a darkness that surrounded the shack, and a sense of sadness and despair was felt by him.

Patch and Indigo arrived together, "What's up Brown?" said Patch.

"This shack," he replied.

"What about it?"

"Well, look at the ground, a lot of people with the same type of sole imprint have been coming to and from this shack."

"So what," said Patch sarcastically.

"Well," said Abraham, "may be those footprints belong to the Germans."

"Maybe," said Patch. "Let's get that lock off and see what's inside."

Abraham stood back and made it crystal clear that he didn't want to be the one to break the lock and go in.

"You big cissy," said Patch as he barged past Indigo and Abraham. "It's just a shack. Wait till you have to fight face to face with a German, what are you going to do then, Brown, shake his hand and say good morning?"

Abraham ignored the remarks and looked on as Patch forced the door open.

The three men stood there and looked inside. Patch entered the dark decaying shack, looked around and said, "Let's see what's under all these covers," and started to reveal the contents.

Indigo stood in the doorway with Abraham directly behind him.

"Look at all this junk," said Patch, and continued to examine the contents. Eventually he found a metal box tucked away in the far corner, and on opening it let out a gasp of surprise. "Gold rings, watches and jewellery," he exclaimed. "Look at it all. Those Germans must have put it all here or known about it. Well, they're dead now so I'll have them." He started to fill his pockets with what he could.

"These are good paintings," said Indigo. "And all this other stuff is worth money, I reckon."

Abraham stood in the doorway. He sensed and felt great sadness about all that was inside, and by now Indigo had been seduced by the gold objects that he and Patch were revelling in whilst filling their pockets. Both men were lost for a while in the powerful grip of greed and want.

"Brown, do you want any?" said Patch.

"No," came the reply.

"OK, suit yourself then."

After a while Patch and Indigo left the shack. Then the three men wandered back to their camp to reflect on their discovery. They talked for a while, speculating as to whose belongings had been locked away in the shack, Patch and Indigo not really caring. They just felt smug.

Abraham wondered why he had been so affected by the shack and didn't really know what was happening to him. But things were changing in Abraham's life and this was just the beginning!

Abraham stood up and wandered over to where the body of Hans Gruman lay, whilst Patch and Indigo decided to inspect their loot. As Abraham looked down at the body his attention was drawn to Hans's left hand, holding what looked like a photograph. Abraham knelt down compassionately by Hans's side and peeled away the dirty fingers from the crumpled photograph. He opened it up and looked in disbelief at it, for there in the photo was an image of the same woman and children as he had dreamt about the night before. "How could that be?" he wondered, and stood up, his injured shoulder tingling lightly. This made him inspect the bayonet wound which was less than a day old, but looked and felt well on the mend. It was as if the healing process had been accelerated somehow. Abraham replaced the photo into the hand of the dead Hans Gruman. As soon as he had done this the tingling sensation in his shoulder stopped, He thought to himself, "How can I explain this to the others? They will just laugh and dismiss it or think that I am going mad. Perhaps I am going mad," thought Abraham Brown. He walked back over to the others who had been speculating as to how many dollars they would make when they eventually got back to America.

Patch looked back at Abraham and spoke. "Hey Brown, some of this jewellery has got names and stuff engraved on it but it's all in French, what do you reckon that's all about eh?"

"Guess this stuff once belonged to French people. Why it's all in the shack here I don't know, but these Germans knew and maybe someone else does, or why would they murder them like that?" replied Abraham.

"Murder!" snapped Patch. "How can it be murder, this is a war."

By this time Abraham was getting used to Patch's aggressive and uncompassionate ways so he decided to say no more.

"Let's pack up and get on our way," said Indigo.

The three of them made for the road, which was about fifty yards away. The truck that the Germans had used had been damaged by gunfire the day before, but Patch had found a map inside which he took as they started their voyage of adventure and life changing experiences.

Chapter Three

Paris had been liberated and the Allies were on their way to driving the Germans out of France. Several groups of German soldiers and individuals had deserted in the south, and Hans Gruman and the other German soldiers had for some time been raiding local villages and farmsteads looting homes of any valuables. They knew that anything of worth would be hidden away by most people, so they would often torture or even kill anyone who did not immediately hand over gold rings, jewellery and so on. Hans Gruman was the most vicious of them all, often showing no mercy to man, woman or child. Their plan was to gather as much loot as possible, then bury it and retrieve it sometime in the future, after the war perhaps. The shack was their temporary store for all their loot.

Abraham had sensed the pain which each item gave off, reflecting the terror from the rightful owners as they were tortured or killed.

The shack still contained some paintings and the like, but these were too big to carry so they were left. The allure of gold had seduced and satisfied Patch and Indigo's thirst that day.

German High Command knew that soldiers were deserting or going into hiding, so a very special soldier known as Claus the Giant was sent out to track down such groups, thus stopping embarrassing propaganda and deterring others from straying in their duty to uphold the power and destiny of the Third Reich.

Now just a day away, the German was coming. His real name was Claus Schmidt, he stood seven feet tall and had short blond hair and a scar from a knife fight that went up the left-hand side of his face. He wore a smart grey German uniform that was tailor made and specially adapted for him. On either side of his waist he wore holsters containing a pistol and below that, strapped to the outside of each thigh, a throwing knife.

On his right shoulder he carried a sniper rifle and on his left a tomahawk, which he could throw with deadly accuracy.

In the mid-1930s Claus was German wrestling champion and later joined the Circus Berlin, where he did a strong man act together with knife throwing.

It was when he was with the circus that he learnt and perfected throwing the tomahawk; the one he now carried had taken many lives and his reputation amongst the ordinary German soldiers was well known and feared.

Claus knew about Hans and the others from various reports in the area, and a German reconnaissance plane had taken a photo of them all by the edge of the wood, unloading a truck from looting raids on nearby villages.

Claus's tunic had a bulletproof metal plate sewn into it to protect his heart, one area of his anatomy that he feared getting hurt or injury to. In contrast, he never bothered to wear a helmet but occasionally wore a cap.

As if the threat of him alone was not enough, he had two companions that went everywhere with him. These companions were no ordinary helpers to Claus, but two specially trained Dobermans that stood either side of him. Their names were Death and Destruction.

Often, Claus would starve them before letting them off the leash, as they knew they would be rewarded once they had tracked down their prey and disabled them with their vicious bites.

Claus had trained himself and the dogs to go without food for days.

He served only one purpose – he was a killing machine.

Although well-educated and a speaker of German, English and French, somehow he had evolved into a psychopath and a devoted servant of the Third Reich.

Now he was coming in search of this renegade group, but unbeknown to him, his work – in a way – was already done, as all were now dead.

* * * * * * * *

A wasted journey, or maybe the beginning of a new one? Who had slain the five sleeping Germans and why had Abraham dreamt of Hans Gruman, his wife and sons?

Chapter Four

The three men had walked many miles that day; their legs ached and they knew by the map that a river was nearby. They eventually came to a small humpback bridge and slid down one side of it to refill their canteens. It was a strange feeling to know that people were at war and killing or being killed in the far distance, but for now they just forgot all that and sat by the water's edge.

Patch was first to take off his boots and socks, followed soon after by Abraham and Indigo. As Patch sat on the riverbank he rolled up his trousers and put his feet in the cool refreshing water. "Ah, that's good," he said to the others who were just lying there in the grass looking up at the lightly clouded sky. "Do you think we will get out of this war alive Templeton?" asked Abraham.

"I like to think so," he replied.

"What's your first name, Templeton?"

"Indigo."

"What, like the colour?"

"Yes, I guess so."

"Can I call you that from now on?"

"Sure, Brown, and what's your name?"

"Abraham, call me Abraham."

"OK Abraham, and how about Hancock, what's your name?" he called over to Patch.

"Well, call me Patch, everyone does and don't ask me why 'cos it's pretty obvious by my face, ain't it?" he replied.

"How's your shoulder wound, Abraham?" enquired Indigo.

"It's OK," came the reply, but Abraham just kept quiet about it healing faster than normal.

Abraham and Indigo chatted for a while and then catnapped in the soft grass while a gentle warm breeze flowed over them.

Even Patch relaxed and smoked his last cigar whilst his toes danced happily in the cool clear river. As he lay there he reflected on his unhappy childhood, and remembered a rare time when he and his father had gone fishing back home, when Patch was ten years old.

His father almost seemed human that day even though he drank as he fished. It was probably the only time his father had ever praised him. That day a few other families were fishing and bragging about the fish that they had caught there in the past, full of themselves and bravado.

There they were fishing with their homemade rods. Patch's father was just about to say, OK that's it for today, let's pack up, when suddenly Patch's bait attracted an enormous fish. Once the hook had cut into the fish's mouth both Patch and his father battled to land the most enormous fish they had ever seen. Patch's father jigged a merry dance around the fish whilst saying, "Well done son, well done!"

That evening the fish was on the tea table.

His father had praised Patch only once and now this French river had brought that memory flooding back to him, he laid back and smiled. In his heart he wished that should he ever be a father, he would try and praise his son each day in some way, and as his mind was full of such thoughts a tear ran down the side of his face and splashed into the grass.

This was a new emotional experience for Patch.

As the river flowed slowly by, the men – each in their own thoughts – were disturbed by gunfire high up in the afternoon sky.

They looked up to see a Spitfire and a Messerschmitt Bf109 locked in aerial combat.

The Spitfire had a small plume of smoke coming from one of its wings.

"It's a Spitfire," said Indigo, "and a kraut battling it out."

Indigo knew British planes as his father would often comment on the war in Europe before America came into it. His father had a friend back in England who flew Spitfires.

As Abraham looked up at the planes he was struck by the beauty of the Spitfire, its wings all rounded at the ends, such grace, elegance and form. Graceful like a bird. Its curves blending into the sky like clouds. The roar and power of the engine as it manoeuvred through the air trying to avoid the pursuing German aircraft.

How aggressive the Messerschmitt looked in contrast, its engine sounding aggressive, its straight lined contours running along the fuselage and into the wings. The Me109 reminded him of an angry wasp.

The three men had never seen aerial combat before. Their necks began to ache as their heads tilted back to watch the two planes fight it out in a duel to the death. The smoke from the Spitfire became thicker and it started to lose height as it disappeared far into the distance, followed by the Me109 moving in for the kill.

"Poor limey," said Patch.

"What's a limey?" asked Abraham, who had never heard the word before.

"It's what we call Britishers where I live," Patch replied.

"Britishers?"

"Yes, those English bastards."

"Hey, my dad's English so watch your tongue," retorted Indigo.

"What's the difference between the English and the British?" Abraham enquired.

"Some people call the English, Britishers or Limeys, it's all the same really – they refer to us Americans as Yanks in the same way," replied Indigo.

"Yeah!" said Patch. "And didn't the British have an empire a bit like the krauts are trying to get, and didn't they try to kill anyone who got in their way, eh? Answer me that, Mr Smartypants."

Indigo wanted to argue about the differences but knew that Patch had gone into one of his argumentative moods so he said no more.

Minutes before, all three men had been at peace, and now an ugly atmosphere filled the air.

How men's moods could change so quickly. How men's worst enemy, the ego, used them like a puppeteer and would be the curse of mankind forever.

From where they were they could see some large buildings in the distance set in the hills amongst vineyards. They looked at the Germans' map and decided to make their way there to investigate and maybe get food or information about any Allied forces in the area. They gathered up their backpacks and guns; their feet felt soft and refreshed. One by one, they scrambled up the bridge embankment back onto the road.

Indigo looked at his watch. It read three o'clock, and he reckoned they should reach the vineyards within two hours at the most.

* * * * * * *

Meanwhile, Claus the German was half a day from the wood with the shack, where his fellow countrymen lay dead. His companions of pain, Death and Destruction, followed and obeyed every command from the Germanic giant.

* * * * * * *

The three men came to a track branching off the road going up into the hills where a monastery stood. A large wooden cross, five feet high, stood to the left of the entrance and a statue to the right. The statue had been vandalised so much that neither Abraham, Patch, nor Indigo could work out what it was. They agreed to rest awhile and sat by the road's edge.

"Either of you got any cigars or cigarettes?" asked Patch.

"Here," replied Indigo as he passed Patch a rather flattened cigarette whilst lighting up one for himself.

It was half past three in the afternoon. Abraham and Indigo stood up in preparation to go up the track to the monastery when Patch noticed someone on a bicycle in the distance coming towards them. The three men held their German weapons at the ready and crouched down to the side of the statue. The bicycle came closer and closer until it passed them. They looked in disbelief as a young German soldier cycled past. His hair was swept back, his eyes fixed open just staring in bewilderment. He did not blink, but just cycled past them with nothing on his feet, not even socks, his bare feet blistered and sore. Off he cycled into the distance, his mind lost forever, another victim of the insanity and horror of war.

Abraham's shoulder wound ached and he was uncertain about what he had just seen.

Indigo thought to himself, "Poor bastard."

Patch thought nothing and said to the others, "Let's get going."

Off they went, walking three abreast up the steep, stony gradient towards the monastery.

The buildings stood grandly upright in a defiant and proud manner on the hillside as they had for the past seven centuries. The walls around the monastery were now in disrepair and badly weathered. A bell tower stood at the highest point and was rung every hour, day and night, 365 days a year, an achievement that the monks had upheld for the past five hundred years. The monastery housed twenty brothers whose ages ranged from thirty to ninety-nine years old. They were mainly French, but there were also a few brothers from other countries.

As the men approached the entrance to the main building they turned to look back at the most incredible view. The fields were like a patchwork of the most beautiful shades of colour that Mother Nature herself had ever weaved, set amongst a thousand fields of green.

Chapter Five

Sniff, sniff went Patch's enquiring snub nose. "I smell food," he said, "and I mean real food, not that crap we've been living on."

Abraham and Indigo looked at one another and smiled.

The three of them approached the main door, their stomachs becoming noisily excited by the thought of feasting to excess.

Indigo was just about to knock on the large oak doors when a voice came from behind him. "*Bonjour monsieur.*"

The three men turned to see two monks standing side by side, one a large stocky fellow holding a staff and the other very short, to be more precise four foot eight, and holding a sling shot in his right hand.

Both men had bare feet and were dressed in blue robes, the back of each man's shaved head adorned with the tattoo of a blue flower.

"*Parlez vous anglais?*" enquired Abraham.

"Yes but of course," came the reply from the short monk. "Please come with us, we have been expecting you."

Abraham's shoulder wound lightly tingled in the presence of the two monks, which was reassuring as he now had a theory – an idea, a hunch – that if his shoulder ached it was a bad sign but if it tingled it was a good sign. He kept this in mind even though he did not as yet understand it, and would have to wait until his next dream which would reveal the truth about it to him.

The large oak doors opened inwards and Abraham, Indigo and Patch were led down a high ceilinged corridor and through another set of doors into the dining hall.

"Please be seated," said the shorter monk. "I am Brother David and this is Brother John. Our fellow brothers will soon be joining us to eat so please wait and be our guests."

The two monks disappeared through an archway.

"This seems a bit too much 'nice and friendly' if you ask me," said Patch. "My gun is staying next to me just in case."

The three of them looked around the medieval dining hall. They had never seen such an old building or room before. It had a good feeling to it and as the aroma of food intensified throughout the air they became more and more at ease and relaxed, even Patch Hancock!

Dong! the bell in the tower rang out.

Indigo looked at his watch, it was six o'clock.

A line of monks entered from each end of the room and sat surrounding the American guests. Brother David walked over and spoke, "Please dine with us, and if you are in need of a bed for the night then you are welcome to stay, but we can only accommodate you for one day and one night as that is our rule. I hope this is acceptable to you."

They all nodded as the food was brought in. They were served meat and vegetables and were given a glass of wine each. As they ate, the other monks occasionally looked up and smiled at them. This felt an almost surreal experience to the three men.

"Fancy that," said Patch, "wooden plates, that's a first for me."

"And the wine," replied Indigo, "it's like nectar."

Soon they were full up and rubbing their stomachs.

"These monks eat well," Abraham thought to himself.

Then all the plates and tableware were cleared. The monks said a short prayer as they did at the start of the meal and then filed away out of the dining hall. Brother David returned and asked if they wished to stay the night, to which they all nodded instantly whilst smiling.

"Please, come with me to your room for the night."

The three men followed him through what seemed a maze of corridors and stairways until eventually they were shown into a room with four very inviting beds inside. The bell in the clock tower rang again.

"It is eight o'clock," said Brother David. "Please excuse me as I have duties to attend to. I shall return at nine and take you to our Elder Brother Simon. He will answer any questions that you may have."

Brother David left the room, leaving the three men time to settle in and talk. The room had a single arched window, and in addition to the four beds there were two tables, each one with two chairs. The room was cool as all the walls were made of stone and the wooden floor had a thin rug across the middle.

"Don't you think it's a bit too nice here as they let us enter with our guns? Surely that must be very intimidating to such holy men," said Patch.

"Perhaps they are genuine," replied Abraham.

"Yeah, or contacting the krauts right now and telling them that they have three American soldiers as house guests," said Indigo.

Abraham's shoulder tingled lightly. "I think we're going to be all right here for the night," he said. He then went over to the window to look outside. The window faced an inner courtyard where a giant tree stood in the centre. A full moon was now visible in the evening sky and several monks sat on a circular bench surrounding the tree.

Abraham, Indigo and Patch sat and talked with one another. Now that they were calling each other by their first names, their attitudes towards one another had changed for the better.

The bell tower rang out.

"Must be nine," said Abraham.

"Yeah," said Indigo, checking his watch.

"Better leave our weapons in the room," said Abraham, to which the others nodded in approval.

Tap tap, came a knock at the door.

Indigo opened the door and was greeted by Brother David who asked them to follow him to see the head monk, Brother Simon.

One by one they filed out of the room following Brother David down the corridor to the right.

Eventually they came to a doorway and were led into a room set in the corner of the monastery, the highest point in the building other than the bell tower. French doors led outside to a balcony. The walls were panelled in wood and many paintings were hung around the room. From behind a large desk an elderly figure stood up to greet them.

"Welcome gentlemen. I am Brother Simon and am happy to answer any questions you may have."

Brother Simon walked around the table and shook their hands in turn. Firstly Patch, then Indigo and lastly Abraham. When their hands gently grasped one another a warm feeling travelled up Abraham's right arm, across his chest and into the bayonet wound. This was yet another new experience for Abraham.

Brother Simon looked deeply into Abraham's eyes and spoke. "Ah, I see you have the gift, my son," to which Abraham just smiled, not really understanding what had been said to him.

Patch and Indigo just looked at each other, both thinking, "What gift? What's the old man babbling on about?"

Indigo enquired as to how it was the brothers were expecting them, to which Brother Simon explained, "Well, I have a telescope on the balcony just outside those doors. I love to watch the night sky, the moon and the stars, it has always fascinated me ever since I was a boy. During the daytime I sometimes observe things in the distance and earlier today I saw the three of you by the roadside. Nothing more, I just saw you by chance, heading up the track."

Abraham spoke. "I am sorry if we have offended you by carrying guns into your monastery and I hope the other brothers were not worried or afraid that we had come here to harm anyone."

"Well," said Brother Simon, "I observed that when the three of you saw that lost soul cycling along the road you let him pass on his way unharmed, even though he wore the uniform of your enemy. That made me decide that although you had weapons of death upon you, your nature was not one of violence and that you had compassion."

"Please tell us of this place," enquired Abraham, to which Brother Simon explained the history of the monastery.

"We are the Order of the Tree of Life. This monastery was built around the tree that stands in the middle of the circular courtyard and was constructed about seven hundred years ago." He talked for a long time and told them that the tree had healing powers and that a legend prophesies that when the tree dies it will also be the end of humanity.

"What a load of bullshit," thought Patch.

The men talked with Brother Simon until eleven o'clock.

"Please, it is time for me to retire for the night," said Brother Simon.

Brother David led the men back to their room, showing them where they could wash and freshen up.

"Hey, Abraham," said Patch, "what did that monk mean when he said you had the gift?"

"No idea," replied Abraham, playing it down. His destiny was only just unfolding itself to him in a very gentle and subtle way, just letting him know he was gradually changing.

Once back in their room, the three men settled down for the night. In turn, they each fell into the timeless dimensions of sleep, just as the candles flickered their last flames into the room.

Chapter Six

Claus the Giant was nearing the wood where his fellow countrymen lay dead. As the skies were clear and the moon shone brightly he carried on his journey through the night with Death and Destruction at his sides. He was only a few hours away and ready to create hell for anyone who got in his way.

* * * * * *

As Abraham slept, more dreams came to him. The first was of the five Germans, bound and gagged as they slept. Then the figure of a woman approached and one by one slit their throats. She was left-handed just as Indigo had surmised, and although he could not see her face, in the dream he saw that she wore a red headscarf and that the tip of her little finger on the right hand was missing. She was not alone, but her companions were some distance away on the road waiting in a truck.

* * * * * *

The fluctuating sensations of tingling, aching and warmth that Abraham had felt in his left shoulder over the last twenty-four hours had come about in a very strange way, one that Abraham would never know, be shown or be told. As Hans Gruman had become a monster and because he had killed himself, his afterlife would be nothing but darkness and oblivion for eternity. His wife and two sons who all loved him dearly were innocent victims of a British bombing raid. They were of a purer spirit than most people so Hans was given a few brief moments in spirit with his family. This was only able to happen in Abraham's dream and was a very rare occurrence in our earthly existence and world.

As Abraham had been tortured moments before Hans's death, a tiny particle of energy from his spirit had made its way into the bayonet wound and would remain trapped in his shoulder throughout his life.

Abraham would never be able to see into or predict the future, but his dreams would answer many questions and guide him to help others in life.

His shoulder would react to many things and give him a power in life to use only for good.

* * * * * *

As the three Americans slept, Claus the Giant reached the Germans' camp. As he approached his two companions, Death and Destruction, started to go wild as they could smell the dead bodies. Claus tied them up and with his flashlight looked around. He saw the crumped and now decaying corpse of Hans Gruman and then walked around and discovered the five other dead Germans. When he saw how they had been slain he went berserk, for although it was them he had come to punish he felt it was his right and nobody else's. He felt cheated and took it very personally. It was the early hours of Wednesday morning, so he rested for a while and would decide what to do in a few hours' time when daybreak would fall upon him.

* * * * * *

That night, a young British pilot was brought to the monastery by some members of the French Resistance. Although his wounds were serious they were not life threatening. It was thought safer for him to go there than to the village two miles away – the Resistance had received information that in the next day or two the Germans would be retreating through it.

The brothers at the monastery had a reputation for helping the sick and were reputed to be able to perform miracles. The monastery would help anyone in need, but Abraham and the others could only stay one night.

Chapter Seven

At seven in the morning, Brother David came into the room and asked if anyone would like breakfast, to which Patch was the first to reply, "Sure thing thanks."

Brother David went on to say that he would give them a tour of the monastery afterwards.

They all dressed quickly and once more filed out of the room behind Brother David, following him back to the dining hall.

They ate alone as the monks only ate one meal a day and this was in the evening time. Breakfast consisted of cereals and bread, jam and honey and although only water was provided to drink, the three of them were most grateful and enjoyed every morsel of food.

When they had finished, Brother David gave them a tour of the building, finishing in the courtyard where the giant tree stood in the centre.

"What sort of tree is it?" asked Indigo.

"Nobody really knows, but to look at it resembles a mighty oak tree," replied Brother David.

They walked around the tree and came to some branches with leaves that were black.

"Why is this so?" enquired Abraham.

Brother David replied, "It started when the first World War began, and now with this second war the tree appears to be slowly dying. We fear the worst for humanity as the legend says that when the tree dies, life for all humans will die also."

Once again, one thought went through Patch Hancock's mind: "Bullshit".

Abraham reached out with his left arm to touch the darkened leaves of the tree and in an instant his shoulder ached. Then the aching turned to pain in the exact spot where the bayonet had entered his shoulder. Abraham moved around the tree to where the leaves were green and lush. He reached over and touched them but this time his shoulder tingled and became warm, warm in the sense of heat but also in a way that felt so good to him. As he stood there and the seconds went by, he felt as if he was levitating off the ground and laughed out loud in front of Indigo, Patch and the other monks.

"Hey, Brown, are you crazy?" shouted Patch.

"If this is being crazy, then I guess I am," replied Abraham.

Brother David was most intrigued by this, then said, "Gentlemen look over there, what do you see?"

They all looked over to a table where two brothers were playing chess.

"Two guys playing chess," replied Patch in his normal grumpy voice.

"Please, go over to them and ask them to tell you their story," said Brother David.

The three men wandered over not quite knowing what to expect.

Abraham sat down on a bench next to the brothers and asked if they would tell them their story.

Brother Gregor spoke first. "I was a proud German soldier fighting the British who I hated very much."

"I was in the British Army, fighting the Germans for King and country," replied the second monk whose name was Brother Bernard.

Both men had fought against each other in the first World War.

The village two miles away came between the Germans and the British one day. Many, many soldiers died, until only two remained alive; they were Brother Gregor and Brother Bernard. Both men tried everything they could to outwit each other, trying to make the other expose himself for a clear shot. They did not know that they were the last two soldiers left in the battle that day.

Towards the evening a mist rolled in over the village just as the light was fading. Brother Bernard saw a figure moving in the shadows, took aim and fired his rifle. The figure crumpled to the ground and lay there still and devoid of life.

Brother Bernard came out of his hiding place and made his way towards where the body had fallen. He was halfway there when a shot rang out. Now he too lay on the damp grass, his body going into shock as he bled internally from the bullet wound. All was quiet until a woman called out from the nearby houses. "Pierre, Pierre!" she called. A fifteen year old boy had gone out into the evening to try and get food from another house. He and his family were almost starving.

Bernard had mistaken the boy's silhouette for that of Gregor and had mistakenly shot the young boy dead.

As Bernard walked over to the body, Gregor had shot him and he now came out of hiding and walked towards the two bodies. He reached the now dying Bernard and kicked him a few times whilst aiming his gun at him. Bernard was not quite dead, but close enough. Gregor then walked over to the boy's body; by now his mother and the villagers were sobbing at the innocent victim's side. When they saw him approach them they charged at him, hurling insults and thinking that he had shot Pierre. Soon a mob surrounded him, delivering their vengeance upon him by punching and kicking him until he lay covered in blood.

Bernard and Gregor lay on the ground for some time, the life force almost gone from their bodies, ebbing away from them.

* * * * * *

Brother David had been visiting the village before the British and Germans had started to fight from either side of it. He had taken refuge in the cellar of a house where an old friend lived. He heard what had happened to the poor young boy that night and went in search of the two soldiers to see if they were dead. He eventually found them and had them taken to the monastery and placed beneath the Tree of Life, as this was the only hope of stabilising and saving them. Even so, he doubted they would survive as they were both so close to death.

Brother Bernard spoke. "We stayed here until the war ended and then made our way back to our own countries, but could never settle. So we both, without the knowledge of the other's intentions, came back here to live and devote ourselves to healing and meditation."

"Yes," remarked Brother Gregor. "I arrived only a few weeks before Bernard and was here in the courtyard when he entered the monastery through those oak doors over there. We ran to each other and embraced like long lost brothers."

"Indeed," remarked Brother David. "So gentlemen, that is their story, but let me ask each one of you: whose fault was it that innocent Pierre was killed?"

Brother David looked at Patch first who answered without hesitation. "Poor kid. Wrong time, wrong place I guess."

Then Brother David looked directly at Indigo who said, "It was a terrible accident and it was very unfortunate, but nobody is to blame really, it was a mistake."

Brother David then looked into Abraham's eyes and asked him who he thought was to blame.

He answered. "Unfortunately, both Brother Bernard and Brother Gregor are responsible for the boy's death as neither man should have been in a foreign land killing for whatever reason in the first place."

Brothers David, Bernard and Gregor all looked at Abraham and said in unison, "Yes, you are right." A look of great sadness fell upon Brother Bernard, filling him with guilt and remorse as he was reminded of that terrible tragedy nearly thirty years ago.

Chapter Eight

The bell in the tower rang out, it was ten o'clock and in the far distance Claus the Giant was on his way. He had examined where the Germans had been camping and saw the discarded American guns, and from this deduced that there had been a shoot-out a few days before. Whoever killed the five tied and bound soldiers would pay dearly for it.

His companions Death and Destruction would now follow the scent of Abraham, Indigo and Patch. Claus was a gigantic figure of a man and before leaving on the manhunt, single handedly buried his fellow countrymen in a shallow grave.

He was one mean motherfucker at the best of times and was convinced that the Americans were responsible for his countrymen's deaths.

It was the last few days of August, 1944 as Claus started his manhunt.

* * * * * * *

The injured RAF pilot had been placed under the canopy of the Tree of Life.

Indigo, Patch and Abraham were introduced to him and told him about being separated from their army unit and being ambushed by the German looters back in the wood. They asked if it was him they had seen being chased by the Messerschmitt, to which he answered, "Yes, I was way off course and had lost my bearings and direction due to damage to my Spitfire. That Me109 chased me for what seemed like hours but it couldn't have been that long."

"You're lucky to be alive," said Indigo.

"You can say that again, old chap," came the reply.

Abraham asked the pilot about the Spitfire and introduced himself. "My name's Abraham Brown, and yours is?"

"Freddie Richards," came the reply.

"Your Spitfire looked so graceful and natural, like a bird. Does it feel like that when you're flying it?" asked Abraham.

"Oh, yes," replied Freddie. "It's a truly wonderful plane to fly. It's similar to another plane the RAF fly called the Hurricane."

Abraham was an ordinary farmer from Kentucky and had never even heard of the RAF, yet alone its squadrons of Hurricanes and Spitfires.

"How did you get up here to the monastery?" enquired Indigo.

"There were some French Resistance fighters who saw my plane crash and brought me here for safety."

"What, you mean up that steep hill?" said Patch.

Brother David interrupted and said, "There is an easier way to get here on the other side of the hill."

The four servicemen chatted for a while and after an hour Freddie was taken to a room in the monastery to rest.

"Brother David," said Indigo, "I would like to speak to the people who brought Freddie here if that is possible."

"Certainly," he replied. "They will be back later to help pick grapes for our winemaking. Please join us at midday and bathe in our spa pool in the cellars, you will find it most refreshing."

The three Americans nodded and looked at each other in a cautious manner. They went and sat on a bench at a high point just outside the monastery. They all gazed at the endless landscape, occasionally scarred by man's savagery towards one another. This was in the form of craters left by exploded munitions.

As they sat side by side, each of them was deep in his own thoughts.

Abraham's eyes picked out a farm with large grain silos. This reminded him of the day his father was killed when Abraham was just fifteen years old. Now he and his family rented the farmland, making just enough money after the harvests to survive each year. Like so many people worldwide they could never afford to buy the land, and had no choice but to pay a high rent. All their work, year in and year out, made their hearts and souls sink very low, causing much unhappiness. All brought about by the greed of others and lack of fairness.

Abraham became a little anxious as he began to worry about his mother, sister and brother. How were they coping? He was at war, thousands of miles away from his homeland like so many other brave American soldiers sent across the Atlantic to fight in Europe. So many mothers, fathers, sisters and brothers, separated from their loved ones through no fault of their own.

Abraham thought much as he sat together with his comrades. As he gazed at the rich and fertile landscape of France, it all seemed a bit like a dream at times, for if he had been told years ago that all this was going to happen to him in life he would have laughed and never have believed it.

Him, a black man, stuck with two white men in a monastery in the middle of a war – beggars belief!

* * * * * *

Patch was reflecting on his life and thought to himself that if he got through the war alive he would better himself academically, and maybe change his job. He worked as a mechanic in a transport company repairing large trucks. It was a dirty job and a hard one. He wondered how his mother was at that present time and wished he could telephone her just to tell her he was fine.

* * * * * *

Indigo's was thinking of how he could clear his gambling debts back home. He wondered whether to come clean and ask his father for the money to pay off his debts. He reached into one of his jacket pockets and pulled out a gold ring, one that had been taken with all the other loot from the shack in the wood. It was a lovely ring and had French words inscribed on the inside. He wondered what they meant, and started to play with the ring, trying each finger for size. When he reached his little finger it slid on and fitted perfectly so he left it.

* * * * * *

Dong the bell tower rang out. It was midday and Brother David arrived. "Please come with me," he said. They followed Brother David back into the monastery and were taken to a dome shaped room. The ceiling was very low. They were led down a spiral staircase situated in the centre of the room. As they descended in almost total darkness, the surrounding air became cooler and cooler. The staircase ended on a circular platform surrounded by water in a cavern deep under the monastery. The cavern was lit by giant candles and there was total silence. A few other brothers were already bathing and smiled as the American guests arrived.

"Please, remove whichever clothing you desire and enter the water for a while," said Brother David.

With that, they all started to strip down to their shorts and one by one entered the water, expecting it to be cool like the air, but the water was quite the opposite, it was tepid and warm to the touch. Around the edge of the platform, below the water level, the rock had been carved into seats and soon the three men were most comfortable as they sat submerged in the water.

Patch was enjoying this very much. As he looked around he saw Brother David remove his blue robe and stand there totally naked. On his back was a tattoo of the Tree of Life. Patch looked away quickly and was a little embarrassed; he now only had one thought on his mind: *Please don't sit beside me Brother David please.*

Brother David stepped into the water and to Patch's relief made his way near to Abraham to be seated.

"Please, get comfortable and close your eyes and relax. Imagine you are one with the water that surrounds you."

"More bullshit!" thought Patch.

They all sat together immersed in a pool of naked monks. Patch was not feeling too comfortable in this situation.

* * * * * *

Claus the German was getting nearer and nearer all the time.

Chapter Nine

"Tell me about these caverns and your tattoos," asked Indigo.

"Well, the tattoo on my back is fairly obvious. It is a picture of the Tree of Life that grows above this very spot. All the brothers have one, but you have to be here for at least two years before it is permitted. We also have a tattoo of a blue flower on the backs of our shaven heads. Once a year, for just one week, the tree blossoms with a beautiful blue flower which we pick, and infuse the petals to make an elixir to help with healing and maintaining a healthy body," answered Brother David.

Patch's eyes rolled in disbelief, and he yawned and tried to nap.

"And this cavern?" asked both Abraham and Indigo.

"That's a mystery," replied Brother David. "Legend has it that the cavern was here way before the monastery and the tree, so who knows? Some of the tree roots come down this far and we believe that the tree and the cavern are connected way back in time."

While Abraham listened and bathed in the refreshing waters his shoulder tingled lightly, and he knew that he was changing somehow. He sensed the purity and peacefulness of this place and could feel the healing power all around him.

It felt very good to bathe in these waters, thought all three men in their own individual ways, and in what seemed no time at all, Brother David clapped his hands together and all the other monks who were bathing climbed out and started to dry themselves.

Abraham noticed that all the men, irrespective of age, had very strong physiques, together with muscles that were incredibly defined.

"Please," said Brother David, "dry yourselves and return upstairs with me. If you are hungry or require a drink please let me know. I am sorry but we are men of peace here at the monastery, and while you have been bathing your weapons have been taken from the room where you slept and have been destroyed."

"Shit!" thought Patch, his mood changing in an instant, and not very favourably towards the monks.

"Please forgive us but this is our way in life. When we return upstairs some people from the village will be picking grapes in the vineyard. They will take you to their village and help you as best they can."

Indigo asked why the weapons were not just confiscated when they arrived, to which Brother David remained silent.

Abraham felt a little unnerved by this action and also remained silent.

As Indigo dressed he noticed that Abraham's shoulder showed no sign of injury from being skewered by Hans Gruman's rifle bayonet. He asked, "Hey Abraham, what has happened to your shoulder and where is the wound from the bayonet?"

Abraham just shrugged his shoulders and replied, "I guess the injury wasn't that bad after all," and carried on dressing, not making an issue of the fact that his shoulder was now totally healed.

When they were ready Brother David led them back up the spiral staircase, emerging into the domed room and outside to meet with the Resistance fighters who were allowed to help with the grape picking. He took them to the top of the main vineyard, on the slopes that led from the monastery down to the road on which the three Americans had travelled the day before.

As they all gazed down, Abraham looked at the road and wondered what had happened to the poor lost soul who had cycled past them barefoot.

Brother David whistled, and a few moments later two men emerged from the vines and walked over towards them.

Abraham's shoulder started to hurt as a third person emerged behind them. It was a woman wearing a red headscarf, and Abraham was reminded of the dream he'd had where the five German throats were cut by a woman such as her.

The woman and two men stood in front of them and one by one shook their hands, starting with Patch, Indigo and then Abraham. The pain in Abraham's shoulder now increased as the woman in the red headscarf stood in front of him and held out her right hand. As he extended his arm to shake hands with her he noticed that the tip of her little finger was missing, exactly as in the dream. She looked him in the eye and spoke. "*Bonjour*, my name is Hélène, and you are…?" Abraham stood there in hesitation to which she asked, "Are you all right? Why do you look at me so strangely? After all, we have never met have we?"

"No, we have not," came the reply. Then after a few moments Abraham spoke. "My name is Abraham Brown."

The others were all looking at Abraham and were thinking his reaction was a little strange. Suddenly, without warning, one of the brothers ran out of the building towards them and approached Brother David. "Brother David, Brother David!" he yelled. "The British pilot has taken a turn for the worse and we are unable to stabilise him."

Unbeknown to everyone, several blood clots had been forming in Freddie Richards's body. They were a result of his injuries from the Spitfire crash landing. Now his body parts were being denied blood flow and he was going into shock.

Brother David started to walk back into the monastery, but then suddenly stopped, turned around and said to Abraham, "Please come with me, Abraham Brown."

Abraham was intrigued and followed him.

He was led to a room where Freddie's vital signs were draining away quickly. The room was known as the Room of Light; in the ceiling was a glass dome with a slightly blue tint within it. The walls were all painted white and the floor was inlaid with a beautiful mosaic depicting swirling patterns made up of the colours in the rainbow.

As Abraham inhaled and exhaled he could smell sweet incense in the air, and a very gentle sound of Tibetan bells could be heard, but as he looked around the room he could not work out where the sound was coming from.

Freddie Richards lay in the centre of the room on a raised platform of warm white stone. There were several other brothers in the room with their hands upon Freddie's body, chanting words in a language unfamiliar to Abraham's ears.

As Abraham entered the room the brothers stood back; his shoulder tingled, then a deep soothing warmth flowed down his arms and into his hands. Without conscious thought he approached Freddie, who was now seconds away from his earthly life coming to an end. Abraham somehow looked beyond the physical form in front of him and ran his hands across Freddie's body until he sensed the areas causing the problem. An aura of light, yellow in colour, flashed from Abraham into Freddie. There was a crackle in the air just like the sound of static electricity, and the room was momentarily filled with a burst of intense but bearable heat.

Abraham stood back and observed Freddie.

Brother David placed his hand upon Abraham's shoulder and spoke softly. "You are truly gifted Abraham, let us wait a few moments to see if your intervention has helped."

Chapter Ten

Outside the monastery, Patch and Indigo asked the two Frenchmen and woman if they had any cigarettes or cigars, and were both highly delighted when they were handed a pack of cigarettes to share between themselves. The five of them chatted for a while; the two Frenchmen were called François and Dominic. They asked both Patch and Indigo all about themselves and told them that in a few hours they would be taken to the village two miles away. There they could stay for as long as they wished.

Dominic said, "The Germans are withdrawing this way and will come close to the village when they cross the bridge that spans the river valley. We know that the Americans are not too far behind them so you have a choice to either stay with us and wait, or risk finding your own way back to the advancing Allied forces."

"We will think about that overnight," replied Indigo.

Patch asked, "Do you have any cigars in the village? I really fancy that and a glass of your French wine perhaps."

The Frenchmen both laughed. "Yes, I'm sure that can be arranged," came the reply.

* * * * * *

Meanwhile, in the Room of Light Brother David walked over to Freddie Richards and spoke gently to him, "Freddie, can you hear me?"

He held Freddie's hand and asked him to squeeze it, which he did almost immediately.

Brother David asked the other brothers in the room to leave, then he took Abraham to see Brother Simon the Elder.

"Please, sit down Abraham and tell me what, if anything, you saw when tending the British pilot," asked Brother Simon.

Abraham was still a little confused about everything, especially his actions, but he composed himself and tried to explain the best he could. He told Brother Simon about the bayonet wound to his shoulder and about his dreams; they were not premonitions but they showed him things which somehow needed an explanation after the event.

"What did you see and experience in the Room of Light Abraham?"

"I saw beyond Freddie's physical body, deep inside, I saw a field of energy which was coloured orange. It filled all the minute spaces between the solid matter that all things are made from. Please can you tell me what I saw?" enquired Abraham.

Brother Simon explained. "What you saw was the human soul, the spirit, the true life force within us all. Tell me Abraham, how did you know where to place your hands on Freddie?"

"The orange glow that I saw was in the form of a sponge, a web that was so intricate and subtle it appeared to have an intelligence of its own. There were a few places that were dark like shadows, and I sensed that these were areas that needed to be attended to."

Brother Simon and Brother David both looked at one another. Then they told Abraham that although they knew of its existence, they themselves could only go by touch, and had never seen the marvel that had befallen Abraham.

"But why me?" asked Abraham. "I'm just a farmer from Kentucky, an American, an ordinary man."

"Abraham, you have overlooked one thing that you are probably not aware of," said Brother Simon.

"What is it?" he replied.

"You have a pure heart, and although you did not seek or ask for this gift it found you, now at this most terrible time in man's evolution."

Abraham was then told that he would not be able to heal or help everybody that he came across in life, but his powers would become stronger and stronger in the years to come.

"I still cannot accept that this is happening to me," stated Abraham.

"Be still in your mind and do nothing, be yourself and let life's journey take you where it will."

Abraham then thought back to the day his father was killed and wished he had had such a power on that day; maybe he could have saved him.

"Let us return to the Room of Light," said Brother David.

Abraham was led back, and as he entered the Room of Light he was amazed to see Freddie Richards sitting upright in the middle of the room.

"What happened to me?" Freddie asked both Abraham and Brother David.

"You developed a slight complication," replied Brother David. "Abraham has helped restore your health and brought balance to the life force that permeates all life on this planet."

"Thank you," said Freddie as he stood up and walked over to Abraham, holding out his right hand in gratitude. As the two men shook hands, Freddie looked deeply into Abraham's eyes and saw great beauty in his soul. Abraham's shoulder warmed gently and he was glad that he had been able to help.

The bell tower rang out – it was three o'clock. Indigo and Patch were now helping outside in the vineyard.

Patch was picking grapes next to Hélène; he felt very attracted to her and although he had no idea of this, she felt the same attraction which she had not felt towards a man in many years. He glanced at her repeatedly and could not help but notice her shapely body, her breasts, her hips and her ass, which moved in such a way that Patch was letting himself become aroused. His hormones were now in full swing and his pupils were becoming more dilated, as they do when one finds another attractive. It was hot outside in the vineyard and Hélène had removed her cardigan, which didn't help Patch with his now raging excitement towards her. As she occasionally glanced at him, she chuckled to herself as she thought he looked a bit like the actor Humphrey Bogart. Patch was making it pretty obvious to her that he was interested.

Indigo and the two Frenchmen were some way away picking grapes and not aware of Patch's excitement.

As Patch picked the grapes he would occasionally pick one out and roll it in his fingers whilst thinking of her breasts.

Hélène could see this out of the corner of her eye, and without knowing it her nipples became hard and erect, protruding out from the tight fitting blouse she wore. She was bra-less and her nipples looked like two cigar butts; Patch loved cigars so this was a bonus!

It was all getting too much for Patch when suddenly Indigo appeared from nowhere and said, "Fancy a smoke Patch?" He held out the packet of cigarettes. "Here, take one."

A huge sigh of disbelief came from both Patch and Hélène – they both looked at one another and laughed loudly.

Indigo had probably diffused a very awkward situation which would have led to much more sexual frustration than the two of them could have coped with.

Chapter Eleven

Abraham appeared outside and called over to Indigo and Patch. "Can I join you guys and help with the grape picking?"

"Of course," came the reply.

He was asked about Freddie's condition, to which he replied, "Oh, he's OK now, or at least he seems to be all right." He could not tell them what had really happened as he feared they would not believe in his powers and abilities.

The afternoon soon went by and the three Americans lost themselves in the simple but satisfying act of grape picking.

Patch stayed close to Indigo and Abraham as he could not handle Hélène being too close to him and triggering off more feelings of arousal.

Patch had no idea that it had been by Hélène's hand that the five sleeping Germans had been killed that night. She and some of the other Resistance fighters had been looking out for them for some time as they knew of their looting raids.

In particular, Hélène wanted revenge, as her mother had died from a heart attack which resulted from Hans Gruman and his renegade soldiers looting her house and knocking her to the floor when she refused to co-operate with them. Hélène had sneaked down from a nearby road that evening whilst her comrades waited in a truck, just as Abraham had seen in his dream the previous night as he slept at the monastery.

Hélène was relieved that the Americans had slept as she had slain the five enemy soldiers.

She did not want to involve anyone else or tell them, lest they think her a cold blooded killer.

She had lost many friends to the invaders from Germany and had no time for sentiment.

She would hopefully keep this secret from Patch and the brothers at the monastery, for if they knew of this murderous act they would not allow her in the vineyards any more.

The brothers accepted Hélène and the other Resistance fighters for what they were trying to do, but her savage act would be unforgivable in their eyes.

It would soon be time to leave for the village. Hélène told them to return inside and say their goodbyes whilst she, François and Dominic waited for them.

Abraham, Patch and Indigo made their way through the courtyard which housed the Tree of Life, and approached the main entrance where Brother David was waiting for them. As they got nearer, Brother David walked out to meet them followed by his fellow brothers. All had clean shaven heads and wore their blue robes. They formed a semi-circle around the Americans and one by one shook hands with them.

Freddie Richards stood to the far right of the semi-circle, and when the three men reached him he said, "Thank you for helping me regain my health, and for saving my life, Abraham."

"Glad I was able to help you Freddie, do you feel your normal self now?"

"Oh yes, I feel great and will stay here for a few more days to regain my strength before working out how to get back to England."

"Will you be able to fly again when you get home?" asked Abraham.

"I don't see why not, but I will probably have to be tested physically and mentally just to be sure."

The three Americans said their goodbyes and came lastly to Brother David.

Abraham's shoulder reacted with a warm tingling feeling, indicating to him that Brother David was a sincere and good man.

They walked out of the courtyard to join the others who were waiting outside.

Freddie and a few of the others followed.

"Everyone ready?" asked Hélène, to which the others replied "yes", and they started to follow the path around to the far side of the monastery, taking them on to the track leading to the village.

The six people grouped together and were just starting on their walk when a voice from below boomed out: "Stop right there or I will shoot!" The six turned to their left to see Claus the German emerge from the vineyard below, flanked by Death and Destruction. The dogs were now hungry for blood!

Chapter Twelve

Back home in America, the lives of families were being shattered as fathers, sons, brothers, uncles and nephews were being reported as killed in action. So many young men with so much to live for being slaughtered in the fight against one man's madness to rule the world. His power and insanity were attracting other evil men to lead his armies in the battle against the Allies, who were fighting this tyranny and evil regime. Brave men from all over the world, black men, white men, brown men, all united in a common fight for freedom and liberty for all.

* * * * * *

Some local society women were driving round to farms and country houses collecting money for the war effort. On this day, six hours behind the time at the monastery in France, they drove up to the farm where Abraham Brown and his family lived and worked. Four ladies emerged from the parked car in front of the house. Their spokesperson was called Sylvia Taylor. She wore a yellow dress, a yellow hat and dainty white shoes. She was a very beautiful woman to look at and had the perfect figure, but on the inside she was selfish and vain and was only raising money to look good in the eyes of other people.

As the women started to walk up the steps to the house, Mrs Brown opened the front door and stepped out onto the porch to meet them. Her hair was tied back and she wore a cotton blouse and working trousers with a red and white chequered pinny tied around her waist. She looked at each of the women in turn and asked cautiously what they wanted. You didn't get many white folks calling at the farm, and this spooked Abraham's mother a little. She noticed how all the women wore fancy clothes and that they all avoided direct eye contact with her.

"Good morning, Mrs Brown," said Sylvia Taylor. "We are collecting money for the war effort, money to help our nation in the fight against tyranny."

"Mmm," thought Mrs Brown. "That's something I have faced many times in my life, in my own country by my fellow Americans."

"Mrs Brown, did you hear what I said?" snapped Sylvia.

"Oh, I hear you lady."

"Well then, please give what you can."

Mrs Brown thought for a moment and then said, "I have already given to the war effort, given more than any money could ever pay for."

"And what would that be exactly?"

"I have given my son, Abraham. God knows why, he is thousands of miles in that direction," as she pointed east, "risking his life for a white man's war."

Sylvia was not expecting that sort of reply, and stumbled as she took a step back. She then said, "Mrs Brown, do you have any money to give or not?"

"No, I do not!" came the reply. "Our harvest was poor this summer and we barely have enough basic things to live on."

The four women stared at her in disgust and turned their backs upon her. One of them whispered something to the others and they all laughed out loud. They walked back to the car, looking around the farm as they did so, thinking of themselves as so much better.

They drove away at speed, deliberately causing the dust to rise as a final insult to Mrs Brown who just stood there thinking about her son Abraham, her heart becoming heavy with worry.

The women had upset her, and she wondered why people were so nasty to others whose skin was a darker shade than theirs. She turned and went back inside the house to carry on with her cooking.

* * * * * *

It was September the first, 1944 and only thirty years had passed since the start of the Great War – the War to end all Wars – how could this ever have happened again?

Chapter Thirteen

Claus the Giant approached Abraham and the others; they had no weapons to defend themselves and stood attentively as Claus emerged from the vines.

"At last, American blood to spill," he said, with a mad look in his eyes. "Which one of you cocksuckers wants to try their luck and make a run for it first, because you are all going to die, you murderous cowards."

"What the hell are you talking about?" replied Patch.

"Oh, you know very well what I mean, American."

"No. I do not."

"You cowards slit the throats of five of my fellow countrymen who were bound and gagged, a day's walk west from here."

"It wasn't any of us, sauerkraut."

Claus laughed out loud and repeated his question. "Who wants to try and get away first before you all die?"

Patch was now getting a little irate with Claus' questioning and said, "Listen, you motherfucking German, it all happened as we slept, OK. When we woke up, someone had killed them already during the night."

"Lies, American. You called me a motherfucker, well you wait till the war is over and we are victorious, I will go to America and make sure I fuck all your mothers."

Patch took a step forward and immediately Abraham and Indigo, who had been standing either side of him, stepped forward and grabbed a wrist each to stop Patch digging an even bigger hole for himself and the others.

"You, bitch!" said Claus. "Who are you and your two companions?"

Hélène answered. "We come from a nearby village and help from time to time picking grapes."

Freddie and several of the brothers stood close by; amongst them was Brother Gregor, the former soldier from the

Great War. He walked forward past all the others and approached Claus. "Stop right there! Who are you and what do you want?" asked Claus.

Brother Gregor then replied and spoke to him in their native German tongue. He spent several minutes pleading with Claus to believe the Americans and go on his way in peace.

Claus seemed to be responding to Brother Gregor's request; he stood silent for a while and then spoke. "You are a traitor to the cause, to the Fuhrer and to the Fatherland. To this, I have but one answer to give you."

Without hesitation, Claus drew both pistols from their holsters on either side of him. The gun in his right hand he held up to Gregor's head and the gun in his left hand to his chest. He looked Brother Gregor straight in the eyes and smiled, then suddenly *Bang,* both guns were fired simultaneously into the man of peace.

Brother Gregor's body recoiled away from Claus as the others looked on in disbelief. How could anyone be so cruel and to one of their own countrymen?

"Who's next or shall I choose?" asked Claus.

"Go fuck yourself!" shouted Patch, and broke free from Indigo and Abraham's hold. He lunged forward and charged at Claus.

A single word in German was spoken and the two Dobermans, Death and Destruction, leapt into action as they intercepted Patch's approach. Both dogs flew at Patch and grabbed an arm each, their momentum sending him backwards and landing flat on the ground, both dogs holding onto him, waiting for their master's next command.

The others could do nothing but watch in horror as all this was happening. As it did, Brother David had managed to sneak away unnoticed.

Hélène took a step forward and spoke. "I killed your fellow Germans, me and no one else."

She then explained to Claus the events of that night, and why she was motivated to carry out such an act.

"You lie, French whore!"

"No, look." She reached into her pocket and produced a switchblade. "Here, this is the blade that killed those filthy German bastards!" She opened out the knife exposing the razor sharp blade and said, "These are the blood stains from your comrades, still on the knife."

"Mmm, in that case, I have something very special for you," said Claus as he quickly re-holstered his guns and grabbed his two throwing knives. Without hesitation he launched them at Hélène.

They flew through the air, homing in on their targets which were the femoral arteries located at the top of the inner thighs. It was Claus's intention to watch Hélène bleed to death and for all the others standing helplessly by, to witness.

The knives struck home and Hélène fell to her knees screaming in pain, she knew it was her time to die and that if she removed the knives, the blood would pump out of her even quicker. She just about managed to stand and holding the switchblade in her left hand she charged at Claus whilst screaming obscenities at him.

There was a sudden thud and Hélène's skull split wide open as the tomahawk struck, the blade penetrating deeply into her forehead.

Claus loved this weapon the best!

Brother David was now amongst the vines and was getting into position to give Claus a surprise. Patch screamed out at Claus and tried to break free from the dogs that held him, but could not do so. He then turned to face one of the dogs and head butted Death, knocking him clean out. Then he wrestled with Destruction who was snapping ferociously at him all over.

They neared a ledge overlooking the valley and over they went, the dog tearing into Patch as they stumbled. At one point Destruction tore a pocket clean off Patch's uniform; this pocket was full of gold rings and soon they were all dispersed away from him, spinning and glistening in the air as they fell.

"Who is next to die?" asked Claus as he stepped forward over Hélène's body and knelt down to retrieve the tomahawk and throwing knives that protruded from her body. He looked up to see Abraham standing in front of him. He just stared at him as he wiped the blood from the weapons of death in Hélène's clothing. He stood up face to face with Abraham and said, "Ah, the black one, and what shall I do with you?"

Abraham just stood there. He felt no fear, anger or aggression.

Claus then asked him, "Why do you fight for a race of white men who took you from Africa to breed as slaves and now expect you to fight in their war?"

Now, despite an element of truth in what Claus was saying, Abraham knew that not all white Americans were racists and not all Germans were deranged, psychopathic, Nazi killing machines.

Abraham asked Claus what would make him leave them alone, to which he replied whilst licking the blade of the tomahawk, "Only your deaths. Anyway, black man, when we are victorious and rule the world we will liberate you from the white man's oppression."

"And how will you do that?" asked Abraham.

"Oh, it's already started. Other sub-species called Jews are already being exterminated by the thousands each week and in time, your race will either face the same end or be made slaves to the new master race of Nazis."

Chapter Fourteen

Brother David was nearly in position to help Abraham and the others.

There was no sign of Patch and Destruction; Death remained unconscious.

"Enough of this small talk," said Claus as he drew one of the pistols from his holster and then pointed it at Abraham. "How would you like to die, quickly or slowly?"

Abraham stood and looked directly into Claus's eyes. At this moment Claus slowly started to pull the trigger. Suddenly Claus felt paralysed, he could not move. He had looked directly into Abraham's eyes and although it did not affect him as it had Hans Gruman, he now felt a little confused and unsure of himself.

Abraham's shoulder started to tingle a little, just as Claus regained his self-control. Within a fraction of a second of the trigger being pulled, a large round pebble launched by Brother David's slingshot struck Claus in the right temple, instantly knocking him to the ground, joining his dog in a state of unconsciousness. It was reminiscent of the biblical tale of David and Goliath, where David slays the giant with a sling. Claus was seven feet tall and Brother David somewhat shorter at four feet eight.

All the brothers of the Order of the Tree of Life were against violence and aggression, but they were taught to specialise in just one discipline of combat using weapons. This was only to be used as a last resort and to preserve the life of others. Brother David's weapon was the sling; other brothers were trained in archery, fencing, the staff and so on.

Indigo and the others came forward towards Abraham and the sleeping giant; the bodies of Brother Gregor and Hélène were removed back into the sanctuary of the monastery.

Brother David, together with some of the others, tied up the sleeping giant and his death hound whilst Indigo and

Abraham went to look for Patch. They walked over the rocky outcrop overlooking the valley down below and visually scanned every nook and cranny looking for Patch.

"We're going to have to climb down there," said Indigo.

"Yes, you're right," replied Abraham. "You go down on that side of the rocks and I will go down on this side."

The two men made their descent along a rocky and stony tract, which was a border at one end of the vineyard.

"Over here!" shouted Abraham, to which Indigo responded by making his way over to him.

"Look Indigo, there's blood on this rock and it looks fresh."

"Yes I agree, so maybe Patch is around here somewhere."

* * * * * *

Patch was not far away but was hidden by several large rocks; the dog Destruction had tried to rip him apart leaving him in a bad way. As he lay there on his back he looked up at the sky and slowly drifted into unconsciousness, into a world halfway between this and the next.

He felt light as if he was floating, and soon found himself sitting on a riverbank next to his father.

"Hello Patch, I've been waiting for you, please don't be afraid."

"I'm not afraid Dad, in fact I feel as I have never felt before. Am I dead?" he asked.

"No Patch, you are visiting my afterlife and will return to your body in less than a second, but here it will feel like a lot longer."

"I don't understand, why am I here?"

"Listen to my story son, and always remember it until we next meet."

His dad passed him a fishing rod and together they sat in the timeless dimension beyond worldly life. He explained to Patch how he was beaten as a child and treated so cruelly by his own father.

He went on to say, "You see Patch, when you were born I had already started to drink. As you grew up you reminded me of my own childhood and I just could not cope with that, so instead of being a good father to you I just drank more."

"Why didn't you tell me this Dad, when you were alive?"

"You were so young Patch, and it would not have been fair to you to know of such things."

Patch remembered seeing his father one day without his shirt on, and on that day he had asked his father what all the scars on his body were, to which his father said nothing but just glared at him.

This explains a lot, he thought to himself, so he asked his father a new question.

"Dad, were those scars on your body the result of your beatings as a child?"

"Yes Patch, I hope you kinda understand now that other people and events changed me in childhood."

"I understand now," said Patch as they sat and continued fishing for a while.

"Dad, what sort of fish are we trying to catch here?"

His father laughed and said, "Lost souls. You see son, I must help others that were like me, then sometime – not so much in the future or at a specific time – there will be a moment when I will go on to my true afterlife. There, I will wait for you and your mother to be with me once more to live a proper family life in the way we never did."

Patch could now see in his own self so much more than words could ever say.

"Son, the only time I ever really praised you was when you caught that fish, remember?"

"Yes Dad, I have never forgotten."

Both men put down their fishing rods, stood up and embraced one another. The love they felt for one another was more powerful than an atomic bomb, more beautiful than a thousand sunsets.

"Remember this moment son, and in another time and place, this feeling will be eternal between us."

"I love you Dad."

"I love you son, and I must go now, please take care of your mother."

"I will Dad," and with that Patch's spirit returned to his body.

Chapter Fifteen

Abraham and Indigo heard a groan of pain and discomfort. They looked over to where the sound came from and rushed over to where Patch lay, hidden by the large rocks. Patch opened his eyes and as he looked up he saw two faces staring down at him, one black and one white. "Where am I?" enquired Patch.

"You're on the slopes of the vineyard," replied Abraham. "Don't you remember the fight you had with that dog?"

"Oh yeah, I remember all right, where is that hound from hell?"

"Don't know Patch, we haven't seen it in our search for you. Do you think you can sit up and stand?"

With that, Patch sat up and wondered to himself if he really had seen his dad or if it had been a dream. He said nothing of it and asked to be helped to his feet. Abraham and Indigo stood either side of him and helped him up.

"I ache all over," said Patch, "and look what that kraut dog has done to my clothing." He felt for his pocket that had been torn from his jacket. "All those rings have gone, and to be honest I'm glad," Patch announced, which surprised his companions. "Easy come, easy go I guess." Then he remembered the murder of Brother Gregor and Hélène. *Shit,* he thought to himself, and then enquired what had happened to Claus the Giant.

"Oh, he's safely tied up next to his other dog for now," said Indigo. "They are both out for the count."

The three men chatted for a while and as Patch spoke both Abraham and Indigo noticed a subtle change in his persona, and a good one at that. They also noticed something different in his face. Patch usually wore a frown, and his forehead would be full of lines which showed his stress and repressed inner feelings. This had all gone away now and he looked fresh and worry free.

There was now a deep bond developing between the three men, one which they all sensed and welcomed.

Abraham felt reborn after his experience with the bayonet, and now Patch also felt reborn after the out-of-body experience with his father. He would eventually accept this and come to terms with it.

"Let's get back up the slope and join the others," said Indigo, to which the others nodded in agreement.

Abraham and Indigo held Patch's arms and helped him as they climbed back up the slopes of the vineyard. Slowly but surely they clambered up to the top and walked to the pathway that surrounded the monastery. They walked over to where Claus had been tied up, only to discover that he and his death hound were nowhere to be seen. All that remained were the ropes that had bound him. His loyal canine killer had returned after his attack on Patch Hancock and bitten through the ties around Claus's wrists and ankles.

Oh shit, the three men thought at once.

"That means that psycho Nazi is out there somewhere," said Indigo.

"Yeah," replied Patch. "Maybe I will be able to have another try at giving him a good thrashing in a fair man to man fist fight."

"There's no such thing as a fair fight with that guy," replied Abraham.

The three men made their way to the monastery entrance and were met by Brother David.

"Are you all right?" he enquired to all of them.

"Yes," replied Abraham. "Do you think it possible for us to stay an extra night here? I know it is not usually permitted."

"Certainly," replied Brother David, who went on to explain that the two Frenchmen, François and Dominic, would also be staying and would escort them to the village the following day.

"Please, come and dine once more with us this evening," said Brother David.

Abraham noticed that Brother David seemed quieter than normal, and sensed that he was upset at the tragic loss of

Brother Gregor. "Brother David," he said, "it is a sad day for you I know, to lose a fellow brother in such a cruel way."

"Yes, indeed Abraham, and it is even sadder when it was one of his countrymen that had slayed him."

"Mm yes," replied Abraham.

As they were led back into the monastery many thoughts went through Abraham's mind. He recalled the times in his life when as an Afro-American he had been treated unfairly and discriminated against just because of the colour of his skin, or was it something else? Something in mankind that makes him want to have power or control over others different from himself; to kill, torture or wipe out an entire race of people with that same desire.

Abraham thought deeply, and had often thought that somehow white Americans would one day accept him and his kind to be treated as equals. He was sure of this, but when in the future this would happen only God knew.

* * * * * *

It was the first of September, 1944 and a charismatic, bright and intelligent young man of fifteen is starting college back in America. He too has a vision, just like Abraham. He would come to help more in the fight against racial injustice than any other man ever has; a young man with such passion for justice and peace in society whatever a man's colour, creed or religion. His name was Martin Luther King.

He and his father were both named Michael King, but after a visit to Nazi Germany in 1934, his father had changed their names to Martin Luther King after the sixteenth century German Protestant Reformist. What would he make of Nazi Germany all these centuries later? It is unlikely he would be all that keen on *Herr Hitler*!

Names are strange things; just labels for individuals.

Abraham's mother and father had also named him after someone famous, who had also lived in Kentucky; his name was Abraham Lincoln.

Chapter Sixteen

Claus the Giant had fled after being knocked out, but would not let the matter rest, so he went into hiding not far away together with his two hounds from hell, Death and Destruction.

He made camp for the night in the valley below keeping the monastery in his sight. He decided to feed his hounds, so he set out some snares in the hope that a rabbit or some animal might become trapped. He attached a bell to each snare and settled down for the evening. His head hurt and was full of ideas about getting even and causing further pain and suffering to the three American soldiers.

Claus noticed that Destruction had been clawing at his mouth a lot so he decided to investigate. He commanded the dog to sit still and proceeded to examine the dog's mouth, which when fully opened revealed a large tooth at the back surrounded by something shiny. Claus got out his knife and levered the object out of Destruction's mouth. He held it up to the light of the camp fire and knew it was heavy for its size, but did not realise what it was.

When Patch and Destruction had wrestled as they fell down the steep and stony slopes of the vineyard, the dog had bitten into one of the rings when the pocket containing the jewellery had become torn away from Patch's uniform. The ring had been wedged and re-shaped over a tooth in the dog's mouth. Destruction had been biting hard that evening to try and dislodge the ring but this had only pushed it further over the tooth where it stayed until now.

Claus just looked at it and did not realise what it was. After a while he threw it away up into the night air where it travelled spinning upwards and then fell to the ground.

All of Patch's rings were now lost and forgotten; easy come, easy go.

Chapter Seventeen

Back at the monastery everyone was sombrely partaking of what would otherwise have been an excellent hot meal of chicken and rabbit pie.

The three Americans were quite shocked by the events of the day, and after dinner they spoke with the British pilot, Freddie Richards, before retiring to their room for the night.

As the three of them lay on their beds, one by one they thought of home and life back in America.

Patch broke the silence and spoke. "Do you think these Nazis will ever win the war?"

"No," replied Indigo. "They are on the run now I reckon."

"Well," said Abraham, "if the Nazis are like the one we encountered today then I dread to think of them winning this war. Can they really hate other humans so much that they want to wipe out whole races of people?"

"Nasty bastards, these Nazis," commented Patch. "I wonder if we will see any more before we get back to our forces?"

The three weary men's minds and their thoughts slowed down as one by one they fell asleep.

The night air was fresh and cool as they slept. The bell rang each hour as it had done for centuries but this did not disturb them, nor the occasional toot from a pair of owls making conversation in the dimension of darkness.

Now as mankind would sleep, creatures would inhabit the land and live their nocturnal existence undisturbed and free from human activity.

* * * * * *

Claus was awoken by the tinkling sound from one of the bells attached to a snare. He got up from his slumber and took out a hunting knife from his backpack. As he made his way to the snare he was watched eagerly by Death and Destruction. Claus disappeared out of sight of the two dogs for a few minutes and returned with a large adult rabbit. He skinned the animal and soon had it cooking over the fire, the two dogs salivating heavily as they watched their master by the fireside. When the rabbit was cooked to his liking Claus divided and cut up the animal into three equal shares. The two dogs ate their portions and afterwards licked the bones from the animal for a long time.

Claus settled down again for the night, he could awake in an instant and be ready to fight or cope with any situation that could arise. Although he had no love of anyone or anything in life (except the Fuhrer) he had respect for his two canine servants and treated them always as equals when it came to food.

It was midnight and a new day was dawning – the day was the second of September, 1944.

* * * * * *

Abraham had many dreams that night and was changing deep within; he was now able to see beyond the physical realm we inhabit and had the gift to heal with his touch.

Chapter Eighteen

The village and nearby monastery kept in touch twice daily via carrier pigeon. News of Hélène's murder had shocked her friends and her sister who now mourned her loss.

The Germans would be retreating past the village any day and the people there lived in fear. Some of the residents remembered the brutality in the last war; the people of France had suffered greatly at the hands of the Germans.

At six in the morning the bell in the tower rang out and the three Americans all awoke. They sat up on their beds and looked at one another. There came a knock at the door; it opened and in walked Brother David. "Time to go, gentlemen," he said.

Abraham, Indigo and Patch dressed quickly and gathered their belongings. They were taken to meet up with François and Dominic to leave the monastery by way of an escape tunnel that surfaced a hundred yards away from the rear of the building and faced the village down below.

"What about Freddie?" enquired Abraham.

"We are waiting for a reply from the British," replied François.

They all said goodbye to Brother David and entered the tunnel. It was high enough to stand up in and soon the men emerged and were on the old track leading to the village.

It was lucky for them that this was an alternative route, as the main entrance to the monastery was being closely watched by Claus the Giant who had risen at first light and had his sniper rifle's telescopic sights aimed directly at the entrance. Claus knew of the village but only had knowledge of the roadway which was marked on his map. He had no idea of the other route that the three Americans had taken.

He would wait a few hours and then proceed to the village together with his canine companions. He had laid out all his weapons on the ground and had been checking the sharpness of the blades on his knives and tomahawk. He cleaned and reloaded his pistols and finished off the remaining water in his canteen, giving the dogs a share each. He would find a stream to refill it on his travels that day.

Claus emptied the remaining contents of his backpack and came to a small radio transmitter. He checked to see if it was still in working order. This gave him an idea how to flush out anyone within the monastery. He radioed his command HQ giving them the map reference and co-ordinates for the monastery. He made himself comfortable, turned to Death and Destruction and smiled.

He had his high powered rifle ready and tapped his fingers impatiently upon the butt as he waited for a response to his radio request. Half an hour passed; the faint sound of an aircraft could be heard.

Claus looked up high in the sky directly above the monastery. A Luftwaffe dive bomber was screaming its way downwards through the sky towards the place of peace and healing. This was an aircraft fitted with a siren underneath, it was designed to strike fear into the innocents it was about to kill. This machine of death was called a Stuka, and the pilot was sighting his bomb on the monastery as it dived down closer and closer towards its target.

Claus watched as the plane released its bomb and manoeuvred out of the dive and into the distance in the direction it had come from.

The bomb fell and struck the bell tower; as it exploded the ancient bell fragmented into a thousand pieces of bronze as the force of the explosion tore into it.

The whole monastery shook and mayhem ensued for a brief moment as the brothers feared for the safety of the Tree of Life. The brothers knew that Claus was still at large and all knew to assemble in an underground safe room until any immediate danger had passed.

Chapter Nineteen

Abraham and the others looked back at the monastery as they approached the village. They stood helplessly on the outskirts as they heard the siren of the Stuka and watched the cowardly attack.

"Shall we go back?" said Abraham.

"No," replied François. "That would not help and only put us in danger. We are at the village now and will send a message to the monastery by pigeon. If there is no reply by this evening then maybe I will return alone to find out what has happened."

They entered the village and walked along the road, looking around as they followed the two Frenchmen. It seemed deserted but after a while they noticed curtains moving and people looking out from inside the houses. There seemed to be an atmosphere and feeling of great unease around them.

Abraham's shoulder ached and he knew that great sadness had befallen the people who lived there.

Most of the village had been damaged in some way or other thirty years earlier in the last war.

They approached the far end of the village and were taken to a farmhouse a few hundred yards from the rest of the village houses. As they approached, the front door opened and a woman stepped out onto the porch. Her name was Emmanuel and she was the half-sister of the now deceased Hélène.

The two Frenchmen nodded their heads at her and entered the house followed by the Americans. They entered a large room in which seven men sat at a table playing cards. The room was filled with the smoke from their cigarettes; this aggravated Abraham's breathing, even Patch who smoked cigars found it a bit overbearing. One of the Frenchmen stood up and spoke to François and Dominic. "Are these the Americans that you want us to shelter?"

"Yes, let me introduce you. This is Abraham Brown, Patch Hancock and lastly Indigo Templeton."

As they shook hands, the Frenchman noticed the ring on Indigo's little finger and enquired as to where he had got it.

"Oh, I can't really remember," replied Indigo in a rather obvious and defensive way, which fuelled the Frenchman's suspicion about his answer.

"Come through to the back of the house," said François, and led them to a room in which they could stay as long as necessary.

"What about the American forces, are they near to here?" asked Indigo.

"They are getting nearer, but between us and them are Germans and they are all over the place; they are on the retreat and very, very dangerous."

François showed them where the toilet and bathroom were and said they were free to go where they liked, inside or outside of the farmhouse. "I must go now with the men in the other room and find out exactly what the Germans are up to. Emmanuel will cook for you later and I will send a message to the monastery and find out what I can." He then went back to the front of the house.

"They were a mean looking bunch of men in that room," said Indigo.

"Yeah, they even made me feel a bit uneasy," commented Patch as they settled into their new surroundings.

Chapter Twenty

Claus's plan to drive people out of the monastery and into the open had failed. As he was deciding what his next course of action would be, a bell rang out from another snare. *Ah,* he thought to himself, *breakfast for me and my companions.*

Soon another rabbit was cooking over the fire, and once again three equal shares of meat were eaten by Claus, Death and Destruction.

He removed the other snares and packed up ready to make his way (the long way round) to the village. His first priority was to go to the nearby stream where he filled up his canteen and washed. The two dogs played in the shallow area and afterwards sat attentively awaiting their master's orders.

As they started their journey, Claus looked up high to where the bell tower once stood, and smiled; he was an evil bastard at the best of times.

* * * * * *

Up at the monastery the all clear had been given and the brothers emerged from the cellars to inspect the damage and clear up.

Freddie Richards felt sorry for the brothers, as they were men of peace and their sole purpose in life was to help and heal the sick and live off the land. He asked if he could help with the clearing up and this request was most welcomed and accepted by the Brotherhood.

Thankfully, the Tree of Life seemed undamaged with the exception of several branches and a lot of leaves being blown away. Several large pieces of the fragmented bell were now embedded into the trunk and it was decided to leave them in situ for the moment. Freddie and the brothers worked continuously for several hours, clearing rubble and making minor repairs.

The plane that had bombed them was a Junkers 88 Stuka and had only used one of its bombs on the monastery. Luckily it was one of the smaller ones that the plane carried. If it had been the largest one much more damage would have occurred. Not only was an air powered siren attached to the underside of the plane used to strike terror into its victims, but as if that were not enough, even the bombs had cardboard sirens fitted to them. As they fell, their scream would be the last thing the prey would hear before being blown to smithereens.

It appeared to their enemies that only the Nazis were demonic enough to devise such terrors. They seemed unstoppable. And they had human weapons like Claus the Giant.

Claus had temporarily been put out of action by Brother David, a man half his size, but a man who used his brain against the brawn of the giant. They say that the pen is mightier than the sword and maybe it is; after all, despite Claus's armoury of weapons he was knocked to the ground, knocked out cold by a simple piece of stone – a pebble.

Claus had not noticed the slight degeneration in his sight or the hardening lump where the pebble had struck his temple. A thrombosis was slowly forming in his head.

Before he set off to the village, Claus had used his radio transmitter to inform HQ of his intention to go there and was now on his way.

* * * * * *

François, Dominic and the Resistance fighters from the farmhouse had gone to see how far away the Germans were. Some reports said two days and some just a day, so they were meeting with some other Resistance fighters in the area to try and get a more accurate picture of what was happening. The American forces were really hitting the Germans hard as they retreated and it was difficult to predict the outcome. When the retreat would finally reach the village was of great concern to the residents.

There were two roads leading from the bridge that spanned the river valley, one was a direct route heading east and the other went through the village where both roads then merged.

The residents of the village envisaged the Germans destroying their already fragile homes as they passed through.

Chapter Twenty-One

The three Americans felt uneasy in the room they had been given and decided to venture outside and explore. They walked back through the old farmhouse.

"Looks like everyone's gone," said Indigo.

"Yeah, but let's watch each other's backs here. I didn't like the way those Frenchies looked at us," replied Patch.

"I hope Freddie and the brothers are OK up there in the monastery," said Abraham. "Let's hope they send us a message via the pigeons and let's hope the pigeons survived that cowardly attack."

Patch made some observations as they walked through the farmhouse. "What a dump," he said. "It's such a shithole of a place, is it really worth saving it from the Germans?"

The old Patch was waking up and emerging, gradually forgetting the out-of-body experience with his father the day before. His mind was starting to dismiss it as a dream. Then Abraham spoke to him. "Last night I dreamt of two men fishing together, a father and a son who found each other through spirit, far outside this physical word. All the hurt through life melted away and was replaced with love, peace and understanding."

Patch looked shocked. *How could Abraham have known of it?*

"Have I been talking in my sleep?" said Patch.

"No, Patch, on the contrary, I am the one who dreamt of the meeting between you and your dad, as you lay there injured between those rocks back at the vineyard."

A wave of emotion flowed over Patch and he fell to his knees whilst tears flooded from his eyes. Now Patch knew it had all happened. The hurt he had felt through his childhood which he had carried into adulthood, the pain, was now exposed to the truth and it simply melted away in an instant.

Patch and Abraham had both now experienced an amazing transformation in their lives. They would look and appear to be as before, but now deep down within both men a peace and calmness had emerged, giving a clarity and freedom from life's harshness.

"What's all this about?" said a rather confused Indigo who did not have the faintest idea of what his new buddies were experiencing.

Patch stood and said, "I will explain to you some time, Indigo, but not at the present. I need time to come to terms with it myself."

The three men approached the front door and exited the house.

"Where shall we go?" said Patch.

"Oh, let's just walk and see where it takes us," replied Abraham.

Indigo was scratching his head in disbelief as to what he had just seen and heard. They had obviously gone mad, he thought to himself, and it's my turn next. He laughed out loud and the others looked at him. With that they all laughed and smiled at each other.

"Oi!" shouted a female voice. It was Emmanuel collecting firewood for cooking from a store at the side of the house. "Where are you all going?" she enquired.

"Just going for a walk," replied Indigo.

"Lunch is at twelve," she said. "If you need me before that I will be in the large barn milking the cows."

"OK," they replied and walked towards the houses in the village.

"I would love a cigarette now," said Indigo. "How about you Patch?"

"Yeah, anything, cigarette, cigar, pipe I don't care," and then Patch suddenly thought to himself, *I don't know if I really do want a smoke.*

As they passed one of the houses the front door opened and an old couple emerged out onto the street; they looked tired, thin and their eyes showed fear in them. They spoke no

English so tried to communicate with the Americans by smiling and holding out their hands.

The men walked over and shook the couple's hands, and as Abraham did so his shoulder hurt and he knew something terrible had once happened in their lives.

These were the parents of the young boy Pierre, who had been mistakenly identified and tragically shot by Brother Bernard in the Great War. Although the couple spoke no English they looked at the three Americans with a glint of hope in their eyes, and repeated "thank you" in French time after time. In their hearts they hoped for an end to come soon at this time, the world's darkest hours.

Several other villagers came out to greet the three guests. One old man spoke to them in English and asked if it was true that the Americans were sending tens of thousands of troops to help free France and drive out the Germans.

"Oh yes, it is true," said Indigo and he went on to tell the old man the rumours he had heard before being captured. "Do you have a cigarette?" asked Indigo.

"No, *Monsieur* I do not, we hardly have any food, let alone luxuries like cigarettes."

The three men walked around for a while and then turned back and headed towards the farmhouse.

Chapter Twenty-Two

Emmanuel was in the barn and had started to milk the cows; she did not hear the barn door open behind her or the seven foot tall psychopath enter.

Emmanuel was an attractive woman, she was thirty years of age but looked nearer forty. Her life had been a hard one. She was almost six feet tall and as strong as most men. Her hair was jet black, her eyes brown and her skin was tanned and typical of southern France; her complexion was healthy and without blemish.

She was the half-sister of Hélène – same mother, different father.

She had experienced several lovers in her life but they had all turned out to be not the nicest of men, using her mainly to work for them or purely for sexual pleasure.

The cows became restless as Claus crept up upon Emmanuel; the smell from inside the barn hid the aroma of sweat that emanated from the German. He got to within a few feet of her, stood erect and coughed to get her attention.

Emmanuel thought it was one of the Americans and without turning her head, said, "Make yourself comfortable and I will be with you once this bucket is full," and continued milking the cow.

She wore a white blouse, black trousers and black leather boots.

Claus chuckled to himself and then spoke. "How about I make myself comfortable between your legs."

Emmanuel immediately spun round and stared at the giant. "Who the fuck are you and what do you want?" she said, knowing immediately who he was but not wanting to make it obvious to him, as it may give him ideas about the whereabouts of the three Americans.

"That's not very friendly," replied Claus. "You said to make myself comfortable, so what better than to let you please me in whatever way I see fit."

"Go fuck yourself, krout!" she yelled.

With that, Claus approached her after commanding the dogs to wait by the barn doors. As there were animals in the barn he did something he had never done before and tied up Death and Destruction. He did not want to be disturbed whilst alone with Emmanuel.

She didn't know whether to tell him that the woman he had butchered outside the monastery had been her sister, but decided to keep quiet and play it cool.

"Well, you French whore, are you going to make me comfortable or shall I persuade you in my own special way?"

Emmanuel had no idea how to get out of this appalling situation or how to escape; she did not know if there was anybody nearby who could help her. She knew that Abraham, Patch and Indigo were exploring the village but did not know their exact whereabouts.

"What's the hurry?" she said in an attempt to try and stall his intentions.

"Listen, bitch, when we are the masters of this puny nation all women will freely give themselves to us, or they and their families will be executed."

"Then you'd better kill every French man, woman and child."

"If necessary, we will," replied Claus.

"But it's impossible to kill everyone."

"Oh, you think so do you? Have you heard what we are doing to the Jews?"

"I have heard rumours, but people are so horrified by the stories that surely they can't be true."

"Oh yes, they are true all right, we are exterminating the Jews already and when they are eradicated, the next race we choose will share the same fate."

Emmanuel was not easily shocked but this was too much even for her to take in. She started to think that Claus would have his way with her.

"Very well, I will let you take me, but let's sit and talk a moment, we women need this sort of thing. Why don't you get those nasty weapons out of the way and then we can get to know one another better."

Claus very cautiously removed his weaponry and placed them to one side.

"You're a good looking man," said Emmanuel as she sat next to him and ran her fingers through his hair.

Claus knew she was up to something but didn't quite know what, so went along with her actions.

She looked into his eyes and drew her head closer to his in preparation for a kiss. She then kissed him passionately, exploring his mouth with her tongue in the hope that he would reciprocate. This excited Claus and he drove his tongue into her mouth in an aggressive and dominant fashion.

Emmanuel chose her moment, and then – without him having any idea of what was about to happen to him – she bit as hard as she could into Claus's tongue. The German screeched out in pain and frantically felt his tongue with his fingers, examining the extent of the damage to his mouth.

Whilst he did this, Emmanuel reached over and took a pistol from Claus's holster lying nearby.

"How does that feel, you Nazi bastard?"

Claus was in a state of shock and found it impossible to reply as his mouth was full of blood.

"Now you piece of German shit, do you know who I am?"

Claus shook his head from side to side.

"It was my sister you murdered up there at the monastery, and now I will avenge her death."

Claus started to back away, his two canine companions barking and trying to break free of their restraints in order to help their master.

Emmanuel held the pistol in her right hand, she outstretched her arm and with Claus standing only a few feet away said, "Time for you to die, you bastard!" She aimed the gun at his heart and pulled the trigger.

Bang! The gun fired, making all the cows in the barn run wild. Emmanuel was knocked to the ground as one of the cows she had been milking ran into her, the force of the animal sending her flying. This winded her and she lay on the ground next to Claus.

The dogs barked aggressively but were tied up; the cows were on edge and in a very confused and volatile state.

The three Americans were making their way back to the farmhouse when they heard the shot and started to head towards the barn.

"Let's be careful," said Indigo. "I mean really careful. We don't have any weapons and I don't want to get too close to anyone who is using a gun, for whatever reason."

"You're right," said Patch and Abraham.

"Do you think it's Germans?" enquired Patch. The other two shrugged their shoulders and they made their way to the barn.

"I recognise those dogs barking," said Patch.

"You don't mean that giant German's dogs," replied Indigo.

"Sure do, how could I ever forget after one of them tried to rip me apart up there in the hills?"

The three men cautiously got to the barn and were not sure what to do next.

"Let's find a window or something to look inside and check out what's been happening," said Patch.

The three men spread out in search of an opening. Abraham checked out the back whilst Indigo and Patch checked down the sides. As Indigo searched his side of the barn he noticed a damaged plank on the side wall, it had a hole in it measuring about the size of a hand. It was eight feet up from the ground. He signalled for the others to come to him.

He pointed to the hole and whispered to the others that he would get up on Abraham's shoulders to look into the barn and investigate. As he was climbing up, Abraham tripped over a large piece of iron and both men fell to the ground with a thud. Patch looked on in disbelief and put his hands upon his head. Both men tried again, but this time Patch helped and made sure that Abraham did not topple or fall over.

Indigo peered into the barn. He saw that the dogs were tied up which was an instant relief to him, he noticed the cows were very restless, and lastly he saw Claus and Emmanuel lying on the ground.

Chapter Twenty-Three

Since being hit by the sling shot, Claus had not really taken much notice of his injury although he had noticed a swelling where the pebble had struck. Deep down in an area of his brain a blood clot was slowly forming and depriving the area of blood. This part of the brain was dying slowly, but now his condition had been accelerated by Emmanuel who had almost bitten his tongue off. It had made him so angry, more angry than he had ever been in his life, making his blood pressure go through the roof. The blood clot had now broken into two halves and was causing Claus brain damage.

Emmanuel had shot at Claus's heart, but unbeknown to her his special uniform had a bulletproof chest plate built into it. He had been shot at point blank range and the force of the bullet, together with the dizziness and disorientation from the trauma now occurring in his head, had knocked him over.

After taking in the scene, Abraham and the others decided to enter the barn so they approached the door and tried the latch slowly. It moved easily, so Indigo slowly opened the barn door outwards, tentatively watched by Patch and Abraham. The dogs were now quiet, almost docile, and as the door was opened fully the cows calmly pushed their way outside into the open.

Patch grabbed the other door and opened it. The three men looked in and at the far end of the barn saw Emmanuel, who had now regained her composure and was standing up.

Abraham's shoulder tingled lightly during these events; this told him that any real danger to him had passed.

The three men walked slowly side by side towards Emmanuel; Claus lay silently on the ground, face up and conscious but not speaking or moving.

Abraham asked what had happened, so Emmanuel told him of the events which led to her shooting Claus. He had bled a lot from his tongue and this was affecting his breathing as he lay on his back; his tongue had swelled and he started to choke. Emmanuel stepped forward and kicked him. "Get up, you murdering bastard!" she shouted.

The three Americans walked closer towards her and Claus.

"He's choking," said Abraham and knelt down towards the giant. "He's too heavy to get up to his feet so help me get him on his side." Indigo and Patch reluctantly knelt down beside Abraham and they rolled Claus onto his side thus allowing the blood to drain out of his mouth.

"Why are you helping him?" said Emmanuel.

Indigo and Patch stood up immediately whilst Abraham looked deeply into the German's eyes and saw the damage that had occurred in his brain. Abraham placed his hands either side of Claus's head and knew that he would never be a danger to anyone again. He looked up at the others and said, "Please wait a while and I will explain to you all what has happened."

Meanwhile, Death and Destruction remained calm, almost mentally detached from anyone else in the barn.

"I want to get my revenge and kill him," repeated Emmanuel.

"Please wait and trust me," said Abraham as he looked at her, this time catching her eyes with his. As he looked at her, she could tell by his face that he knew something other men did not, so she waited silently with the three Americans.

After half an hour, Abraham turned and spoke to Emmanuel. "We are all sorry for the loss of your sister, and understand your need to avenge her death, but now something has changed and I must ask you just one question."

Indigo and Patch looked at one another not knowing what was coming next.

Emmanuel still had hold of the gun and was ready to use it again. "What is it then?" she said impatiently. "What's this all about? Tell me!"

Abraham knelt down and helped Claus to his feet. As well as the obvious injury to his mouth, his face looked different and he wore a blank expression.

"Come on, tell me then!" Emmanuel demanded as she raised the gun to point it at Claus's blooded face.

"Would you kill a child?" asked Abraham.

"What the fuck are you on about?"

"Would you kill a child?" he repeated.

"No, of course not!" came Emmanuel's impatient reply.

"Then this is the dilemma you must now face. This evil man has changed and now has the mind of a child. He has also become a simpleton and it would appear that the part of his brain that was full of hate and evil has now died. He is brain damaged. I think this was probably the result of him being struck in the temple by a pebble."

"Are you sure, Abraham?" enquired Patch.

"Do you not trust me yet, Patch?" replied Abraham.

As Patch searched his head he thought *no,* but in his heart he did, so answered "yes."

Abraham then turned to Indigo and said, "Do you trust me, Indigo?"

"Yes, I do," he replied, as he remembered the day they sat by the river and decided to use Christian names to address each other. That day Indigo had noticed something different about Abraham, not his hair or anything physical, but he had felt a deep stirring within himself. It was a good feeling and one that most men do not experience in life.

Abraham then said to Indigo, "Go and untie the two dogs."

"But Abraham, they are killers!"

"Trust me."

Indigo walked over to the dogs and cautiously released them. The dogs slowly made their way towards Claus, making constant eye contact with him as they did so. When they reached their master, he bent over and patted them on the head. He then gave a garbled laugh which was due to his tongue being severed. The dogs kept staring at Claus in a confused way and both licked his blooded face. The others watched rather nervously. Suddenly the dogs both turned and walked back towards the open door. Upon reaching it they looked back at Claus for a few moments and then both ran off into the distance.

Emmanuel put the gun down and said, "Are you sure he is not just pretending to be like this?"

"No, he is as he looks and is now trapped in the mind of a simpleton," replied Abraham.

After a discussion they all agreed to keep Claus locked in the barn until a decision could be made as what to do with him.

Emmanuel still wanted to kill him, but Abraham had for the moment convinced her not to.

She had seen something in Abraham that she had not recognised in a man before, and became very curious about him. "Come to the house and I will make lunch," she said.

They all returned to the farmhouse and sat talking whilst Emmanuel prepared the food.

Chapter Twenty-Four

At the monastery the brothers had tried to go back to their normal daily routine. A small hand bell was rung each hour to carry on the centuries old tradition. The Brotherhood had received a message from the village by pigeon and had replied.

Freddie Richards was eagerly waiting for the British to get him back to England.

Brother Gregor was to be buried in two days' time along with Hélène. There was a graveyard just outside the monastery's west wall; this was divided into two, one side being for the burial of brothers of the monastery and the other for villagers and outsiders.

* * * * * *

The Resistance fighters from all over the area had met and discussed whether they should help the Allies by attacking the Germans as they approached the village. Many of them were against the idea as they feared severe retaliation for their actions.

The American forces had thought about bombing the valley bridge to stop the Germans getting away, but decided that if they did this they would face the problem of crossing the river and thus delaying any further advancement. The Americans needed to drive on eastwards to meet up with other Allied forces in their mission to drive the Germans out of France.

The leader of the Resistance in the village was called Picard; he was ruthless, which he had to be as they was no time for sentiment in this bloody war.

* * * * * *

Back at the farmhouse, lunch was ready and Emmanuel served the three Americans their food as they all sat at a large oak table. The plates were chipped and cracked, as were the cups.

"Eat up while you can," said Emmanuel. "Some days there's hardly anything to eat but you are lucky today. We only have a few cows now and some chickens, as food for the whole village."

"What is the name of this village?" enquired Patch.

"Since the last war it has had no name. It was decided to do away with it when it was virtually destroyed and abandoned the last time the Germans invaded."

"But you must call it something," replied Patch.

"Yes," answered Emmanuel. "I do, I call it hell."

The others looked shocked by this but then each one of them had sensed it felt different from anywhere they had ever been before.

To come from the very positive, happy atmosphere of the monastery to this village was, to say the least, rather depressing. It was like one minute being in a happy, colourful movie and then being hijacked and placed into a depressing black and white film. Everything about the village was grim; the houses, the streets, the people, the whole caboodle.

At the table, Patch was sitting opposite Indigo. Abraham sat opposite Emmanuel; she looked up at him and asked, "What is life like in America, Abraham?"

"Oh, it's wonderful." Then he paused for a moment and went on to say, "Unless of course you happen to be black, like me!"

Patch and Indigo felt rather embarrassed and awkward, and pretended they were not listening.

Abraham was just playing them along, and then continued. "I love my life with my family in Kentucky, I consider myself a good American. My dad loved it too and named me after one of its Presidents – his name was Abraham Lincoln and as a boy he too grew up in Kentucky. He wanted slavery abolished and for us Afro-Americans to be treated fairly."

"I hear America is a great place, so maybe I will go there one day, when these Germans are gone and we are living our lives in peace once more."

"What about some food for the kraut in the barn?" said Indigo.

"He can live on water for now," replied Emmanuel.

The others did not argue with her answer.

"Is it true that my sister Hélène killed five Germans as they slept by slitting their throats?" she enquired.

"Well, she did admit to it just before she was killed," commented Patch.

All went quiet around the table until every morsel of food had been eaten. After they had chatted for a while, Abraham offered to clear the table and wash up. Emmanuel agreed to this and asked him if afterwards he could go outside and chop up some logs for the fire.

Patch and Indigo decided to go down to the bridge, and took two of the three guns they had taken from Claus when leaving the barn. Indigo opted for the rifle and Patch took one of the pistols. They gave Abraham the remaining pistol and set off to explore the valley, bridge and river as this would soon be a very important strategic place for the Germans and Allies to cross.

Abraham washed and cleared up the dishes and then told Emmanuel he was going outside to chop up some logs for her.

"Ok," she answered. "I will bring you out a drink later."

Abraham went outside to begin his labour. He was used to hard physical work at the farm back home and was enjoying this chore as it reminded him of the home life he was missing so much.

The axe was large and heavy, but Abraham found the work easier than most men as he was conditioned to it, having a very strong but agile body. After a while he began to get hot so he removed his shirt and vest. His body glistened in the afternoon sun; his muscles were well defined. He started to whistle a tune that his father had taught him; he had been told that it came with the first slaves from Africa who had been his ancestors.

Emmanuel heard the whistling and curiously looked out from the window overlooking Abraham. She opened it and asked if he was ready for a drink.

"Yes please, that would be good," he replied.

She looked at his body and thought it was the best she had ever seen in a man, strong and well defined but not over muscular or threatening. As she closed the window she yelped as a splinter from the frame pierced deeply into her right hand. Abraham looked up at her and wondered what the noise was. She held up her hand in the window to show him the wound. He immediately signalled to her that he was coming into the house.

Abraham hurried towards the house and once inside called out to her.

"Where are you?" he shouted, as he could not work out which room she was in.

"In here," came the reply.

He made his way to the room, politely knocked on the door, opened it and walked in. The room was not like the other drab and dull rooms within the house, but was clean and tidy and had a few nice items of furniture – a chest of drawers, nicely upholstered chairs, a small table and a bed with a colourful spread upon it.

Emmanuel sat holding her injured hand. She could be as tough and hard as any man but this was one of those things in life that was most unpleasant – a simple wood splinter, although this one was fairly deep.

"What have you done?" enquired Abraham whilst standing next to the bed on which she sat.

"Oh, it's just a splinter, but it's one bitch of one," she said.

"Let me have a look," and with that he knelt in front of her and examined her hand.

"I will have to cut it out I'm afraid," said Abraham. He reached into his pocket and produced a special knife that he had custom built for use back home on the farm. He started to try and remove the splinter from Emmanuel's hand.

"Let me know if it gets too painful," he said.

"Oh, I will," she replied.

Abraham had removed many splinters from himself and his family back home and was soon retracting the splinter from her hand. Whilst he did this, Emmanuel noticed how gentle and thoughtful he was; she had never known this in a man before.

Abraham's shoulder tingled slightly and felt warm. "There you go," he said, "that's a larger than normal splinter you had there, it must have been very painful."

"Oh, thank you," she replied. She looked at his dog tags and enquired what they were. He explained that all military personnel wore them as a means of identification. She was fascinated by this and asked if she could see them, so Abraham removed them and placed them in her hands. She smiled and they both gazed into each other's brown eyes.

"Do you have a sweetheart at home waiting for you?" she said.

Abraham smiled in a slightly nervous way and replied, "No, just my family and some animals."

They both laughed and Abraham placed the dog tags back around his neck and made his way back outside.

Emmanuel made some coffee and took a mug outside to Abraham who had now finished chopping the logs and had put his vest and shirt back on. He and Emmanuel then went and checked that Claus was behaving himself in the barn. On entering the barn they found him playing. He obviously now had the mind of a child and Emmanuel was now convinced that this was true.

Chapter Twenty-Five

Indigo and Patch had wandered down to the valley and followed the river down to the bridge.

"Can we sit here awhile?" asked Patch. Indigo nodded and they both sat on the trunk of an old broken tree. Patch was once more reminded of the fishing trip with his father when he was a boy. Whilst he was reflecting upon this, Indigo was looking towards the bridge and thought he could make out two figures moving around on the underside of the bridge. He grabbed the rifle and used the telescopic sight fitted to it to view the bridge close up.

"Hey Patch, there are two guys under that bridge doing something."

"Are you sure?" replied Patch.

"Yes, here, look for yourself."

Patch studied the men with the aid of the telescopic sight and tried to work out what they were up to. "Let's get closer," he said.

They both crept through the long grass that lined the river bank and got closer to the bridge.

Indigo used the scope again and suddenly exclaimed, "They're krauts and it looks like they're attaching explosives to the underside of the bridge!"

"No way!" replied Patch.

"I'm sure of it, I can see them clearly."

"Better not let them see us or we may put ourselves and the villagers in danger," replied Patch.

"I agree, let's get back to the village and keep a lookout. There may be more Germans around here."

The two men backtracked to the village and were soon at the farmhouse where they told Abraham and Emmanuel all that they had seen.

As they sat in the kitchen the door opened and François and Dominic walked in with Picard, the leader of the

Resistance fighters. He looked at Emmanuel and asked her to make coffee for him. He was in a bad mood as they had lost several men that day.

Indigo approached Picard and started to tell him about Claus and the Germans under the bridge.

As he did so, Picard suddenly grabbed him with one hand around his throat and pinned the unsuspecting Indigo to the wall. With his other hand he reached down and raised Indigo's hand, which wore the gold ring on his little finger. "I will ask you only once more, where did you get this ring, you American piece of shit?"

"Leave him alone!" snapped Emmanuel.

"Stay out of this bitch!" came the reply.

Patch and Abraham stood up and walked over to the angry Frenchman. "Please let him go," said Abraham in a compassionate tone.

"Why the fuck should I?" came the reply.

"We are your allies and here to liberate France," stated Patch.

Picard let go of Indigo, watched nervously by François and Dominic; they liked the Americans but out of fear did not let it show. Picard then told them what was on his mind. "I don't like Yanks or the English but I respect the British, at least they stood up to Hitler when he invaded Poland. What did you Yanks do? I will tell you what you did, you waited years and now all this time later you think you're the only ones winning in this shit war."

"It's not exactly like that," said Indigo.

Picard then went on to say what was really on his mind; he had heard that a cousin of his who lived in Paris had been raped by an American soldier, and now stories were being told of how some of the liberators thought they could do exactly as they wanted. This had struck a nerve deep within Picard. He grabbed Indigo's finger adorned by the gold ring and said, "This ring has an inscription around it. Do you know what it says, Yank?"

"No," came the answer.

The atmosphere was now very tense in the room and everybody felt very uncomfortable with the situation.

"These rings were given to only a few brave Frenchmen after the last war, Frenchmen who carried out heroic acts whilst fighting the Germans. So how is it you have one on your finger?" He produced a knife from his pocket. "Take it off now or I will cut off your finger."

Indigo removed it in an instant and handed it over. As he did so Picard uttered two words, "Fucking Americans," and then again asked where he got the ring.

Abraham stood in front of the ranting Frenchman; he made eye contact with him and asked him to sit down as he would explain everything to him. Abraham's shoulder ached a little and he knew that Picard was a very dangerous man indeed.

Picard reluctantly sat down as Abraham started to tell him about the shack where the rings were found, and how Hans Gruman and the renegade German soldiers had been raiding homes and taking whatever they wanted. As Abraham was finishing the story, Indigo reached into a large pocket in his uniform and produced the other pieces of gold jewellery, placing them on the table.

"I would not have taken them if I had realised at the time that the people they once belonged to had suffered at the hands of those Germans."

"Mm, maybe so," remarked Picard. "But to me you are no better than those krauts. Now let me see this Nazi in the barn."

They all left the farmhouse and walked out to the barn, where Picard saw for himself the now demented Claus. "What's all that blood around his face?" enquired Picard.

"He stuck his tongue in my mouth so I tried to bite it off," replied Emmanuel.

"Good job it wasn't his dick!" remarked Picard.

All six men in the barn squirmed at that idea. Picard could be one vulgar sod at times.

"You did right not to kill him, I've heard about this heartless bastard and we may be able to use him at a later date to trade or bargain with the Germans. I will go and have a look at the bridge later with François and Dominic, and assess what's going on in those Germans' minds and try and work out when, or if, they intend to blow up the bridge."

They checked that Claus would be fine for the night and locked him in the barn, leaving bread and water. Once outside, Indigo asked the three Frenchmen if they had any cigarettes, to which François replied, "Yes." He and Indigo lit up and sat on a pile of timber to enjoy a smoke. Picard and Dominic made their way to where the pigeons were kept to see if any messages had arrived back from the monastery, or from any of the other local Resistance fighters.

Emmanuel went about her chores in the house and as she walked past Abraham she caught his eye and smiled at him. Her whole face lit up with a joyous expression; this had not happened for a very long time.

Abraham and Patch talked about home and how they could best do their duty as American soldiers when the Germans came.

Chapter Twenty-Six

At the kitchen table the six men sat ready to eat a modest meal that Emmanuel had prepared for them. Picard announced that life at the monastery was getting back to normal and that nobody had died in the cowardly dive bomber attack. This was just one message brought by carrier pigeon, he had received another but was keeping this to himself. The atmosphere was still a little tense with the three Americans on one side of the table and the three Frenchmen on the other.

Once all the food had been eaten, Picard told the others that he, François and Dominic would be going into the village and then on to the bridge.

When the Frenchmen had gone, the three Americans, who did not trust Picard, talked and decided that two of them would follow the Frenchmen and the one remaining would stay at the farmhouse with Emmanuel. It was decided they would toss a coin to determine who would go and who would stay. Indigo and Patch both went for tails and lost their call. Abraham chose heads, which he had guessed correctly, and so remained.

* * * * * *

Picard, François and Dominic entered the village and spread out. They went to every home and told the occupants to hide in basements or under the stairs after midnight and to stay there for at least twelve hours. Picard knew that the Germans were only a few miles away but he did not want to tell the three Americans. The Germans would be crossing the bridge some time during the night.

* * * * * *

Emmanuel asked Abraham if he would go with her to check the cows and the fencing that surrounded the farm, barn and outer buildings. They walked together side by side. Emmanuel turned to Abraham and said, "Don't take any notice of Picard, he is not a very co-operative type and is very selfish."

"Oh, I see," said Abraham who had wondered about Picard's behaviour several times to himself and just put it down to the war.

"You see, his two brothers were killed by the Germans and this has changed him."

"Have you known him for long?"

"All my life. He is my cousin but treats me like dirt sometimes."

"And what about François and Dominic?"

"They are friends of the family," said Emmanuel, who then started to recall to herself the time when she was much younger. Family life at the farm, *maman* and *papa*, her sister, aunts and uncles, nieces and nephews. They were all very close and happy, but now most of them were dead. At that moment, an air of sadness fell upon Emmanuel.

Abraham sensed this, reached out and took hold of her hand. "Don't be sad Emmanuel," he said, in such a caring way that it made her stop in her tracks and look once more into his eyes.

"How did you know I felt sad?" she asked him.

"Oh, I just did somehow," he replied.

"Is life really so bad for you back in America?"

"It can be at times."

"Just because your skin is darker than white Americans?"

"Well, it seems that way."

"That's inhuman, not right, how dare they?" she ranted.

"I think that soon, maybe in ten, twenty or thirty years' time, we will be accepted. Maybe after the war, all Americans will acknowledge the sacrifice made by all men irrespective of the colour of their skin. Surely they will."

Emmanuel agreed as they walked, still holding hands, and eventually they returned to the farmhouse.

Once inside, Abraham enquired about her hand. "How's that hand now?" he asked.

"Oh, its fine thanks."

"Good, that was a big splinter. Please, let me wash up the dishes."

"Ok, thanks Abraham," replied Emmanuel. "I am going to clean the bathroom if you need me."

Emmanuel made her way down the passageway and started her chores.

Abraham washed the dishes, and as he did so started to whistle the tune his father had taught him.

Emmanuel could hear this and smiled to herself as she carried out her work.

When Abraham had finished washing up, he poured himself a glass of water and drank it. After a while he called to Emmanuel, but hearing no reply he decided to go the bathroom to make sure she was all right. He walked along the passageway and looked into the bathroom. She wasn't there, so he carried on along the passageway to the room where he had removed the splinter from her hand earlier that day.

The door was open and Emmanuel was sitting on the bed looking at some old photos of her mother, father and half-sister Hélène. She looked up at him and spoke. "Please come and sit next to me."

Abraham made his way towards her and sat with her as she showed him the photos.

"When will this war end, Abraham?" she implored him.

"Listen, you are safe here with us. Nothing's going to hurt you while I'm about," he stated, in a firm and reassuring manner. He asked if he could wash and shave, so Emmanuel went and found him a razor, a bowl and water jug and a clean towel.

Abraham made his way back to the bathroom, and as he did so Emmanuel asked if she could watch him shave, as she had never watched a man do this before. Abraham agreed and placed the bowl and water jug down on an old table in front of himself. There was a broken mirror on the wall with the bottom right corner missing. He poured some water into the bowl.

"Shall I get you some more water?" asked Emmanuel.

"Yes, sure," answered Abraham.

She left the room carrying the jug.

Abraham took off his shirt and vest and lay them over a chair; he made up some shaving soap and started to shave. The room was poorly lit, making it difficult for him to see exactly what he was doing.

When Emmanuel returned with the replenished water jug she placed it on the table.

"Why is this room so dark?" he asked.

"Well, I guess it wasn't designed for people to shave in," she giggled. "Why not finish shaving in my room, there is plenty of light by the window."

"I've nearly finished now, so is it really worth it?"

"Well, you don't know when you will get another chance to shave in a little comfort," she replied.

Abraham was easily convinced, and now with the help of Emmanuel moved everything out and into her room. He set himself up once more, watched by an intrigued Emmanuel.

"Is that better?" she enquired.

He nodded approvingly. As he continued shaving, she once more marvelled at his physique, this time from behind him.

Chapter Twenty-Seven

Abraham had the perfect body in Emmanuel's mind. He was finding his shave much more satisfactory here than in that dark space and poor excuse for a bathroom. He was using quite a small mirror to shave with and could not see behind him, as Emmanuel started to undo the buttons on her blouse and remove it. She then went on to remove her ill-fitting bra, leaving her shapely breasts to hang freely in the air.

Abraham was finishing and washing his face off. As he stood up straight to dry his face she walked towards him. "Stand still," she commanded him, "and don't turn around for the moment."

Abraham didn't have a clue as to what was happening, but complied with her simple request.

"Close your eyes and tell me what you feel." Emmanuel walked slowly into his back until her now highly charged and excited nipples touched him lightly.

He felt their warm touch but did not immediately realise what they were.

She shook her shoulders from side to side so her nipples brushed and tickled across his back.

She stood there and undid her trousers, dropping them to the floor, and then removed her panties.

Abraham now realised what was happening. He had never been with a woman before and would try his best to keep this from Emmanuel.

She stood behind him, his eyes still closed, her nipples dancing on his back. She reached out and guided his right hand to the soft triangle of hair that adorned the gateway into her inner chasm of sexual pleasure.

A new feeling was surging through Abraham's body, one that he had never experienced before. Although he had developed a deep spiritual power in the past few days, that was now pushed aside by the animal desires taking over his whole self.

"Open your eyes and turn around," she instructed.

As he turned to gaze upon her nakedness he looked into her eyes, deep with desire for passion and sexual love, her lips ready to explore wherever she could, her mouth and tongue ready to give and take pleasure unreservedly. His eyes then saw the most beautiful breasts any man could ever wish for, each breast tapering to the front with nipples that were so ripe they looked like strawberries ready to melt in your mouth.

She undid his trousers and asked him to lie on the bed. She removed his boots and socks, then pulled off his trousers.

Abraham lay there in just his shorts, excitement and arousal now surging throughout his entire body.

She closed and locked the door, then walked over and drew the curtains. She lay next to him on the bed and they started to kiss passionately. Emmanuel wanted to feel and experience making love with a sensitive and caring man, but also a man who could show a different kind of love; she was sure Abraham could give this to her. She felt an urgent need for this to happen now, as in such a short while the Germans would be passing. Life was too short and unpredictable to wait for another time or place in the future.

Although the curtains were drawn, there was still enough light for Abraham and Emmanuel to see each other's bodies. They continued kissing for a while and then Emmanuel removed Abraham's shorts and worked her way down his body, kissing and exploring it with her mouth. on the sensual voyage along Abraham's Adonis-like physique, stopping when necessary to tease him with her soft and gentle lips.

Abraham lay there not knowing what to expect next, he was more aroused and excited than he could ever have imagined.

After a short while, she moved and asked Abraham to sit on the edge of the bed. She stood in front of him, her nipples a few inches from his mouth. As they neared him, he took each one in turn, sucking them softly to begin with but with the occasional bearable bite when the nipple would almost ask for it to happen. It was like two perfect strawberries, ripe and ready, protruding from her perfect breasts, succulent and satisfying in every way. After he pleasured her breasts his hands and fingers explored her shapely buttocks, each cheek like a juicy peach.

Now Emmanuel was aching between her thighs, she hungered to be taken.

Abraham stood up and they kissed once more.

They embraced passionately, their bodies becoming one, moving together with each other's desires and needs in the act of love. Although this was Abraham's first time, his manly instincts now guided him in this new experience with the female form. They lay upon the bed together, the frequency of their lovemaking now increasing until ecstasy was attained for both. Emmanuel's hands now clawing at the bed sheets as she climaxed, their bodies now covered in a thin layer of love sweat. Their aroma now mixing with the sweet smell of jasmine which grew abundantly outside the window, always filling the room with its delicate perfume.

Their two bodies lay side by side together on the bed. After a few moments, Abraham gently brushed her skin with the back of his fingers, he caressed her breasts tenderly and asked if all was well.

"Yes, Abraham," she replied, "I feel fantastic. It was unbelievable. I hope you don't mind me starting it all off."

"No, Emmanuel, I don't mind, you are so beautiful in many ways. Thank you," replied Abraham. He was still wearing the dog tags around his neck, and Emmanuel looked at them and asked if she could wear them for a while.

"Sure you can," he said, as he raised them over his head and handed them to her.

As they lay there she played with them in her hand, but before she could even put them on they had both drifted off into a light sleep. Her hand containing the dog tags was hanging over the edge of the bed and as her muscles relaxed, her hand opened and they fell to the floor, slightly under the bed.

Chapter Twenty-Eight

Indigo and Patch had followed the Frenchmen and kept far enough away not to be noticed by them. A German soldier was on sentry duty by the bridge. He had a radio transmitter with him and was guarding the explosives which had been carefully positioned beneath the bridge. Nobody was sure what was going on, but soon the Germans would be retreating over the bridge; they would leave a few soldiers behind to lie in wait for the Americans to cross, then they would blow them sky high.

"They sure don't like us Americans, do they?" said Indigo.

"Who, the Frenchies or the Germans?"

"Both, but I was referring to the Frenchman, Picard."

"Well, I guess they have watched and felt the wrath of the Germans and have wondered why we didn't come into the war earlier."

"I suppose so, but they should realise it's not our fault and up to the politicians to sort out."

Suddenly both men were startled as the sound of gunfire rang out – and it wasn't that far away.

"Let's get back to the farmhouse," said Patch.

"I'm with you there," replied Indigo.

The two men headed back. Picard, François and Dominic also started making their way back to the farmhouse and were going to the barn to check on Claus.

The evening was turning into one of fear and anticipation as to what would happen to the village. Would the Germans bypass the village on the river road, just drive through, or carry out revenge attacks on the village and its inhabitants?

As Patch and Indigo approached the farmhouse they could hear more gunfire in the distance.

In the farmhouse Abraham and Emmanuel were asleep in each other's arms.

Suddenly, a shell could be heard whistling its way through the evening sky towards the village.

It came to ground and struck an old disused garage at the far end of the village. *Boom!* The shell exploded, sending a shudder through the ground striking fear into all the villagers in hiding.

Together with the shockwave, the loud bang rang out through the air and awoke Abraham and Emmanuel.

"What was that?" she asked.

"I don't know," replied Abraham, and with that they quickly dressed. As Abraham stood up his heel kicked the dog tags further under the bed and out of sight.

"Sounded like an explosion to me," he said, "but I don't know if it was a German or American munition."

The two of them walked through to the kitchen just as Patch and Indigo entered from the outside door at the opposite end of the room.

"Did you hear it?" asked Indigo.

"Sure did," replied both Abraham and Emmanuel.

"What shall we do?" asked Patch.

"Let's just wait awhile," answered Abraham.

They all sat nervously around the table as Emmanuel put on the coffee pot.

* * * * * *

The Frenchmen arrived at the barn to check on Claus. On entering, they saw no sight of him and spread out to look.

"Here!" shouted François. The others came over, and there, cowering in a corner, was the giant German scared out of his wits by the explosion at the garage.

"Bring him into the farmhouse," ordered Picard to the two Frenchmen.

They all walked out of the barn to join the others, who were now drinking coffee in the farmhouse kitchen. Picard marched in first, followed by François, Dominic and Claus.

"You Yanks must hide in the barn tonight," said Picard. "If the Germans find you in this or any other house should they enter the village, they will not be pleased and may take out their revenge on the inhabitants." The three Americans agreed. They did not want anyone to suffer because of them being there.

Everyone stayed in the kitchen until nightfall; the occasional explosion of gunfire could be heard nearer to the village than before.

Abraham and Emmanuel's eyes met several times during the evening, their faces lit up and they smiled at each other. Each time, a warm glow emanated from Abraham's shoulder into his whole body. Whilst he had slept next to her he had dreamt of Hélène, who was now at peace and wanted Emmanuel to know this, but Abraham had said nothing, thinking to himself that she would think he was making it up just to comfort her and make her feel better.

"It's time to go," said Picard.

The three Americans went into hiding in the barn. As they left the house Indigo asked Picard about Claus. "We will keep him with us, and if the Germans come into the village this is the first house they will come to, so we will hand him over to them and say we have helped him," replied Picard.

"Do you think they will believe you?" asked Patch.

"Why not? We'll say we found him wandering on the outskirts of the village and that we have looked after him since."

"Well, I hope that if they do come they will accept that explanation," replied Patch.

Picard told them not to leave the barn on any account and that he would return and give the all clear once the Germans had passed through.

* * * * * *

In the monastery high up in the hills, Freddie Richards and the brothers looked down upon the valley which now lay in darkness. They hoped that the Americans were safe, and as they watched the valley they could see flashes of gunfire followed shortly by the sounds of war.

Freddie turned to Brother David and asked him if he thought the others were safe.

"Yes, Freddie, I am sure they are safe, and will soon be reunited with the American forces once the Germans have fled."

Chapter Twenty-Nine

Throughout the night the Germans crossed the bridge, and once over it took the river road avoiding the village. The villagers were huddled under their houses and in cellars almost too scared to breathe. Young and old living in such uncertainty – could this be their last evening alive?

In one cellar a small boy turned to his mother and whispered in her ear, "Will God come this time and save us *Maman*?" Her eyes were full of despair as she desperately tried to think of an answer. She kissed the small crucifix hanging from her neck and begged to God in her heart, pleading not for herself, but for the child as were so many mothers on this night.

"How can this be happening?" an old man thought to himself, remembering the horror of thirty years ago. "Maybe there is no God for us," he thought, "and this is truly hell." He, too, begged in his breaking heart, full of fear and worry. He felt as if someone had pushed their hands into his chest and was tearing it in half.

How had man become so callous towards his brothers and sisters, all living in the same world? All were born naked, breathing the same air, drinking of the same waters, feeling the warmth of the same sun, all now lost in a new worldly madness inflicted on humanity by the Nazis. Were they once not happy, innocent children, playing as do all the world's young life forms, or were they never like us, but were created by a demon set on revenge for all the human race to suffer?

* * * * * *

As the hours passed, peace and quiet returned to the village. People started to relax a little, many slept, albeit not the most restfully.

In the farmhouse, Claus sat in a chair, his hands tied to it. Picard, François and Dominic sat resting, occasionally nodding off for a few moments. Emmanuel was in her room, the door locked, and as she lay on the bed looking up at the ceiling she felt happy to have had such a wonderful experience with Abraham. She was totally satisfied with their lovemaking, something that all other men had failed to do. She was touched by his tenderness to her after they had both climaxed. He emanated peace and goodness and she wished that they could meet again in the future, perhaps after the war. They could go to a nice restaurant together and enjoy a good meal and a bottle of wine, perhaps. She daydreamed for a while longer as the night unfolded, soon making way for daybreak to visit and start a new day.

Picard, François and Dominic never took guns into the farmhouse or the village, because if the Germans came at any time they may not be quick enough to hide them, so they kept them hidden just outside the village. If someone was found to have a gun, they would be shot without question. Picard deliberately did not mention this to the three Americans and did not care.

Abraham, Indigo and Patch had made themselves as comfortable as they could for the night; the weapons they had taken from Claus were at the ready should Jerry pop his ugly head in and disturb them.

The three men would often think of home; they all came from very different backgrounds indeed.

"I wonder what France is like in peacetime?" commented Patch.

"Maybe we will one day return," said Indigo, "and go to Paris and climb the Eiffel Tower."

Abraham was thinking about Emmanuel; he had not noticed his dog tags were missing and she had not yet discovered them lying under the bed that only a few hours previously they had made love upon. He could not tell the others about his experience with Emmanuel as no matter how he described it to them, they would never understand the passion and sensuality that they had together created in their nakedness.

The three men were just idling in their thoughts when Patch suddenly said "Let's get out of here!"

"You heard what Picard said," replied Indigo, "we have to stay here. Abraham, what do you think?"

"I think we should try and get near to the bridge. The Germans have rigged that bridge with what looks like explosives, and we owe it to our advancing forces to work out how to stop the Germans destroying it before our troops get to cross over."

Suddenly Abraham's shoulder started to surge with pain, so much so that he partially collapsed. He knelt down, bewildered as to the reason for this occurrence. He then started to work out why. Now the bayonet wound was giving him a sign, a warning, and in his mind's eye he could see why. He was helped to his feet by Indigo and Patch and said, "The Germans are not going to blow up the bridge once they have all crossed, they intend to wait for the American troop carriers to be crossing. That's when they will detonate the explosives to kill as many of our fellow Americans as they can."

"Are you sure about this, Abraham?" asked Patch.

"Yes, trust me Patch."

"But Abraham, how can you be sure?"

"I knew about you and your father fishing whilst you lay unconscious in the hills below the monastery, didn't I?"

"Yes, Abraham you did. Ok, let's get to the bridge then."

Indigo just listened; he had not experienced the same strange life changing experiences that his two fellow comrades had, but he trusted them and Abraham's suggestion made perfect sense the more he thought about it.

* * * * * *

Abraham was right, the Germans would let the first few vehicles over the bridge, most likely tanks; their main aim was to destroy as many trucks carrying troops as possible. The Germans had worked out a failsafe to detonation which was to have two sets of detonating wires running to the bridge. Two German soldiers were dug into the hillside, one either side of the bridge at a distance of about two hundred yards from it. These soldiers were hidden by camouflage and were impossible to visually spot, and each was protected by a sniper set high up in the valley offering them additional cover and protection.

Chapter Thirty

As the last Germans crossed the bridge, an armoured car broke away from their convoy and sped up the road into the village. Picard heard the approaching vehicle and stepped outside to intercept it. As it approached the farmhouse he took out a white handkerchief from his pocket and started to calmly wave it, attracting their attention. He did not want the villagers to be put into any danger, and knew that the Germans would not just drive through without stopping and creating some sort of mayhem. The armoured car screeched to a halt, inches from where he stood. A door opened and an officer got out followed by three heavily armed soldiers.

"Do you know the Americans are coming?" he said.

"Yes," replied Picard in an honest and straightforward manner.

"And when they come will you greet them as liberators and spit on the ground when you hear them mention we Germans?"

"I doubt that."

"And why is that Frenchman?"

"I don't care for Yanks that much."

"But you hate Germans, yes?"

"Yes, I hate Germans all right."

"Is it because we are invaders of your country?"

"That, a bit, but mainly because you killed my two brothers."

"Mmm, then you are justified in your hatred of us. And what about the British?"

"Don't like them much either."

"You're a strange one, Frenchman. Now tell me why I shouldn't shoot you or shoot up this village?"

Picard whistled to François and Dominic to bring Claus outside. They walked him over and stood him in front of the German officer who was astounded at the size of Claus.

Picard said, "We have looked after this soldier who we found wandering on the outskirts of the village."

"He wears a non-regulation uniform which is unfamiliar to me," replied the officer.

One of the soldiers stepped forward and whispered into the officer's ear; he had recognised the giant.

"So Frenchman, you have tamed the Beast have you?" The other Germans laughed. "I have heard of our Fatherland's infamous bounty hunter many times, but what has happened to him?"

Picard repeated what he had already said and then, "We found him wandering around and have looked after him until now."

Claus stood there, his mind full of the thoughts of a child. He did not speak and this spooked the German officer. "And what of his dogs, Death and Destruction?" asked the officer.

"I haven't seen any dogs, just him," replied Picard.

The officer walked around Claus several times and then casually returned inside the armoured car followed by his men. The engine revved a few times and then the car drove off into the distance.

The three Frenchmen were not expecting such a response and stood there for a few minutes, nervously expecting the Germans to return.

"Fucking Germans!" retorted Picard. "Let's go and check on the Americans in the barn."

They reached the barn to find the doors ajar and no sign of the Americans inside.

"Fucking Americans!" said Picard. "I told them to stay put until I gave the all clear. They'd better have a good reason for leaving the barn or they will answer to me."

The three men took Claus back inside the farmhouse and called to Emmanuel, who was still asleep.

"Come on, woman!" shouted Picard. "We are hungry, come and get us some food."

* * * * * *

It was light now and seven o'clock in the morning.

Abraham, Patch and Indigo started to fan out and look for anything out of the ordinary beneath the bridge support structures.

The two German soldiers who would detonate the explosives were well hidden and protected by a sniper high up in the hills.

Indigo was armed with Claus's sniper rifle. It was not a standard mass produced weapon but one made to Claus's own personal specifications. Indigo was a trained marksman and made his way along a sheltered ridge on the south side of the river valley. The Germans would destroy the bridge, but only when the American forces were crossing it. Indigo was not sure if he and the others would be able to stop them.

The Americans were now only a few miles away from crossing, they had not anticipated the Germans' retreat during the night. Indigo set himself up at what he thought was a good vantage point, and there he waited for Abraham or Patch to flush out or find the hiding places of the two German soldiers who were now ready to detonate.

As Indigo waited his mind wandered, and led him to think about his life. He thought about all the suffering to humanity that the war had brought about. He vowed to himself that if he got back home alive he would somehow try and help other people in life. For a few fleeting moments he had thought of being like his father and becoming a doctor, but had quickly dismissed the idea as he had never done any serious studying and assumed that it would be too much for him to pass the qualifying exams. His heart was in the right place though.

Abraham and Patch searched slowly and kept low in the undergrowth as much as possible. They each carried a pistol and although both men had experienced a new spiritual dimension in their lives, especially Abraham, they were both prepared to kill or be killed for the greater good.

They had both assumed that only one person would be setting off the explosive charges underneath the bridge, and as each man searched they both tried to get as much possible cover from bushes and the long wild grass that grew in the river valley.

Before starting the search, both men had agreed that they would not venture too near to where the explosives were as they were probably booby trapped to avoid them being disarmed.

Patch was getting a little frustrated as he had just worked out that he had been moving around in a circle, so he sat on the ground and rested awhile.

Abraham was feeling the same, as several hours had passed to no avail in his search.

Indigo wanted a cigarette, his mouth felt dry and he wished he was down by the river to take a refreshing drink.

Patch stood up from his rest; he had nearly fallen asleep, he still felt tired and as he walked he did so in a lazy fashion, dragging his feet. He was just thinking about it being like looking for a needle in a haystack when his left foot hooked something up from the dirt. He shook his foot and carried on walking, but after a few more steps, stopped, turned around and went back. He knelt down to where his boot had got caught up and there, lying in the dirt, was what looked like a wire. He gently lifted up a section. It was definitely a detonation wire; he carefully lifted a few yards more. He had worked out that it was coming from the bridge and running straight past him along the valley slope. Patch checked his pistol and continued to follow the detonator wire, but as he did so he forgot to keep his cover and was exposing his position. As he got closer to where the German's hideout was, he was spotted by the sniper giving protective cover to the German detonators.

As Patch began to close in on the hideout, the sniper's telescopic sight followed his every move. High up on the other side of the valley, Indigo thought he had seen something glimmering in the distance so he trained his scope on the opposite hillside. *There it is again*, he thought to himself.

Although the German sniper was fairly well hidden, Indigo could just about make out the rifle pointing down below. Now he had to make a decision to either keep his gun trained on the

German sniper or lose sight of him and concentrate his line of sight down onto the valley below where he knew Patch and Abraham were desperately searching.

Chapter Thirty-One

At the monastery, Freddie Richards and the brothers had received a message via carrier pigeon and were eagerly awaiting the advancing American forces to drive the Germans out of the region.

Picard, François and Dominic waited in the farmhouse; they had no idea what to do with Claus and would hand him over to the Americans even though now he was no threat.

Emmanuel hoped that she would see Abraham again that day; although she knew it was impossible now, she yearned to be with him once again.

* * * * * *

As Patch followed the wire he suddenly had an idea – why didn't he cut the wire now and then carry on following it, that way the bridge would be safe whatever happened. He got out his knife and started to cut through the wire. The blade cut easily as it was quite thin. Patch carried on following the wire until it started to run above the ground for a few yards and then disappeared into what looked like a square hedge. He stopped and looked down at the ground and noticed that it had been disturbed, and that the hedge almost looked man-made with the use of branches, twigs and leaves. *Was this the hideout?* he thought to himself.

As Patch lay down in the dirt he wondered what to do, then made a decision. He started to tug on the wire until it felt taut, he then gave it one final tug, this time as hard as he could. He was right, this was the Germans' detonator position.

Inside the hideout the trigger unit was pulled from one side to the other. The German soldier hurriedly came out of hiding to investigate. He emerged outside swearing in German and in a state of bewilderment.

There, sitting on the ground right in front of him, was Patch Hancock with a big grin across his face "Hands up Fritz!" he commanded, to which the German immediately put his hands on his head, looking very embarrassed and ashamed of being lured outside so easily.

Patch stood up and shouted in the hope that Abraham or Indigo would hear him. As he did so, the German sniper protecting this hideout was preparing to shoot him.

Patch continued to shout out and attracted Abraham's attention. He started to make his way in the direction of Patch, as he did so a loud *bang* echoed across the valley. Abraham then raced towards Patch.

Bang, a second shot echoed along the hillside. Abraham dropped to the ground, he was Ok, the gunfire had not been aimed at him. He waited a few minutes and carefully set off again to where Patch had shouted from.

The first shot had been the German sniper shooting at Patch, the second was Indigo's response to this.

Patch had been badly wounded, and the German sniper killed by Indigo's marksmanship, an ability which he had not used in a very long time.

As Abraham raced to where Patch lay, Indigo also headed down into the valley to see if he was dead, injured or alive. By the time Abraham reached the spot where Patch lay wounded, the German detonator had fled.

There lay Patch. A large part of his upper back had been torn apart by the high powered bullet fired down upon him. Abraham knelt beside him and knew that despite his newly found abilities and experiences far outside the normal scope of man, he could not save Patch as the wound was too severe and he had lost too much blood.

Abraham's shoulder became cold, and he knew that the life force which exists in all humans was preparing to leave Patch's body. He held on to Patch like a mother would cradle a dying child; tears appeared and ran down his face, he prayed in his heart for the tender grace of God to have mercy upon his soul.

Patch looked up at him, and their eyes met. Just before Patch went to his afterlife, a stillness was felt deep within him, his life flashed before him and together he and Abraham fleetingly saw beyond the realm of earthly human life.

Now the restless tide of breath was no more and his heart, which had played the rhythmical drum beat of life, had ceased.

Patch's earthly life had come to an end.

Chapter Thirty-Two

"Hello, Scott, came a voice. "Back so soon?"

"Dad, is that you?"

"Yes son, it's me."

"Am I dead?" asked Patch.

"Far from it, son, you are alive but not in the way you are used to."

Father and son sat on the riverbank once more, this time in their afterlife.

"Dad, you called me Scott, you never called me that before, I don't understand."

"I can still call you Patch if you prefer, son."

Patch was still a little bewildered, but things seemed to be becoming a little clearer to him.

"Look down into the water, son, and tell me what you see."

Patch looked down into the crystal clear waters in front of him and gasped in disbelief.

"Where's my patch, the brown marks on my face, where are they?"

"They are back in the world you just passed from."

"Is this heaven, Dad?"

"How do you feel, Scott?"

"I feel heavenly Dad."

"Then that answers that question. To be totally honest son, we are as close to heaven as one can get."

"Is there a hell, Dad?"

Patch's father laughed and said, "How can there be a worse place anywhere in time than where you've just come from? War is the nearest to hell that any human can experience anywhere."

Patch understood what his father was telling him: sometimes things are as they are and need no explanation.

"Are you still fishing for lost souls Dad?"

"Yes, son, and soon I will have earned my wings."

"And what will become of me, Dad?" asked Patch who now accepted his new existence.

"You, Scott have earned yours by helping to save the lives of many men."

"Can I stay with you Dad?"

"Yes, son, in a short while we will ascend to our true destiny, in a place of unimaginable beauty and peace. One day your mother will join us there and we will have the life we never had together on earth."

A beautiful radiant light fell upon them both and all was well in their new life for eternity.

* * * * * *

Indigo arrived and knelt down beside Abraham, he placed his hand upon his shoulder and his words were quiet and soulful. "Is he dead, Abraham?"

"Yes, Indigo, I'm afraid he is."

"Poor Patch, he didn't deserve that. He found the detonation hideout and has saved the bridge and many lives."

"He is at peace now, Indigo, and will never know pain again."

"Do you know that for certain, Abraham?"

"Yes, I do."

The two men looked at Patch for a few minutes, and then made sure that the German who had fled was not in hiding close by.

Indigo smashed the detonator unit to pieces with his rifle butt before throwing the rifle into the undergrowth and screaming out loud into the air, "Fucking shit war!"

"Let's get back up onto the bridge," said Abraham. "Help me get Patch up onto my shoulder."

The two men made their way up to the village side of the bridge.

On the far side the Americans would soon be crossing. Neither man could possibly have known that the explosives had been wired in tandem and another German was hidden away ready to detonate once the trooper carriers had started crossing the bridge.

Abraham and Indigo carried Patch's body to where the east road led to the bridge. They laid his body down gently beside the bridge. Abraham took off his jacket and covered Patch's upper body and head. As he did so, his shoulder tingled and felt warm, this was very reassuring to Abraham as he now knew that Patch was happy in his afterlife. Both men sat close to Patch's body and waited.

"Why did he have to die?" said Indigo.

"I don't know," answered Abraham.

"He was changing into a better man, Abraham."

"Yes, I know, I had also noticed it deep within."

"What shall we do now, wait or go up to the village?"

Abraham paused for a moment and then said, "Listen, I hear engines."

They both listened carefully and could make out the noise. They stood up and walked onto the bridge.

"It's a tank, Abraham, and it's one of ours!"

Both men smiled and embraced one another.

"Yes, you're right, Indigo, they're Americans and going after the Germans I guess."

As the tank reached the bridge Abraham felt extreme pain from his shoulder, he yelled out and turned to Indigo. "Something's wrong?" he said.

"What do you mean, Abraham?"

"There is still danger." The extreme pain continued.

"How do you know this?" enquired Indigo.

"I just do."

The tank was now on the bridge crossing over, followed by a second tank, the men inside poised at the ready to blast anything that got in their way.

"Indigo, you walk on this side of the bridge and I'll walk along the other side."

"What are we trying to do, Abraham?"

"Just make your way over and look down at the base of the bridge and see if you see anything suspicious."

The two men slowly started walking over the bridge, one on either side, scanning the ground below them. They took no notice of the tanks as they passed by. The tank crews wondered what the two men were doing but they could clearly see that they were Americans so carried on crossing the bridge.

Chapter Thirty-Three

Down below in the valley the other German lay hidden, ready to blow up the bridge once the troop carriers were crossing. His hand lay calmly on the detonating handle; he would do his duty and follow his orders to the last. He could have blown up the bridge once his fellow Germans had crossed or when the American tanks were approaching, but his officer had given him the last orders and they were to kill as many Americans as possible. This he intended to do with pride and honour.

Abraham and Indigo made their way along the bridge and were nearing the far end. Abraham's shoulder still hurt and he knew there was danger. He called over to Indigo who crossed over to him. Both men shook their heads as they had not noticed anything suspicious below them. Now the first troop carriers were starting to cross over, Abraham walked out onto the bridge and held his hands up. The approaching truck ground to a halt and the driver leant out of the window and shouted, "Hey, what's the idea, fella?"

"What's the problem, boy?" said a Sergeant sitting next to the driver.

Abraham ignored the remark. "You gotta stop crossing over, get your men out and off the bridge."

The trucks were now lining up to cross over, there were far too many to reverse backwards off the bridge.

"Listen, boy, we ain't going anywhere so get out of the way or I will move you myself."

The convoy had stopped and a slight sense of panic had come over the German detonator, so he decided to set off the charges and braced himself ready to carry out his deed of madness. He forced down the triggering handle and waited for the explosion, but nothing happened. For a moment he was confused so he reset the detonation trigger and tried again. The same thing happened – nothing. "Shit!" he thought to himself and quickly made the decision to break cover and follow the wire towards the bridge, checking for any breaks or damage to it. He traced the wire to where it had become damaged somehow, maybe it had been chewed by vermin. The German got out his knife and re-stripped the insulation on the two wires, then twisted them together to complete the electrical circuit once the plunger was reset and fired.

Indigo called over to Abraham and the two American soldiers from the truck. "Quick!" he shouted. "Look, there's a kraut down there and he's doing something."

The Sergeant looked down and ordered the driver to get his binoculars from the truck.

They all looked down into the valley watching the German as he repaired the wire. The Sergeant took the binoculars and started to focus them to where the German was. "Yeah, you're right," he said. "There sure is a kraut down there."

"Then get your men off the bridge now before he sets off the explosives," said Abraham.

"What explosives is that, boy?"

"The ones underneath your feet that will be set off any moment."

"Holy shit!" came the reply from a now very flummoxed and embarrassed Sergeant.

The Sergeant and driver went back along one side of the bridge, shouting at the troops to get out of the trucks and off the bridge, whilst Indigo and Abraham did the same on the other side.

The German was now on his way back to his lair of evil, eager to destroy the bridge and anyone on it.

Abraham looked back over the bridge as they got to the end and safety. He could see what looked like several children coming onto the bridge from the other side.

The tanks that had previously crossed had split up, one taking the valley road east and the other going through the village. Some of the villagers had come out from hiding to see the tank, and they started to cheer at the liberating American forces. Some children had run down to the bridge to welcome the following convoy; these children were now running onto the far end of the bridge.

Abraham shouted to Indigo to stay with the Americans, everything was in a state of chaos as the troops sensed they were in danger. Abraham was a fast runner and fired himself towards the oncoming children, his shoulder hurting badly once more. He reached into his pocket and produced the pistol that had once belonged to Claus; he knew he would not reach the children in time, certainly not to get them off the bridge safely so he stood in the middle of the bridge, took aim and fired the gun towards the oncoming children, making sure that his aim was too high to put them in any real danger.

Indigo and the Americans watched from a now safe distance and could not quite work out what Abraham was actually doing, as from where they were it looked as if he had gone mad and was now shooting at the village children.

All this was happening in a split second; by the time Abraham had fired the third bullet all the children were running back off the bridge, screaming as they went.

In this split second when everything was happening at once, the German's hands pushed down on the detonator. "Third time lucky," thought the soldier, as he carried out his orders to the last. The electrical current produced by the detonating unit raced out along the wire at the speed of light. It travelled two hundred yards to the base of the bridge and up to where several bundles of high explosives were positioned underneath it.

BOOM! The charges exploded with incredible force sending concrete and steel flying out in all directions – and somewhere amongst all this was Abraham. The ground shook for miles. Indigo and the Americans looked on in horror as a large section of the bridge disappeared, plummeting down into the valley below, creating a massive dust cloud.

All the villagers came out into the streets. Picard, Emmanuel, François and Dominic hurried out of the farmhouse to investigate. High up in the hills the monastery shook a little due to the blast. Freddie and all the brothers felt most concerned as to what had just happened.

Chapter Thirty-Four

As the dust settled, the German solider looked back as he fled from the scene, he felt proud of himself for the destruction he had caused and did not know that he had incurred only one casualty in this murderous act.

On the village side of the bridge the children were now being comforted by their mothers and fathers.

Picard and the others from the farmhouse arrived to find a priest knelt praying next to Patch's lifeless body. Picard knelt down and lifted the jacket covering his face. Even he, being a man hardened by war and made almost heartless, was sad to see that it was Patch Hancock lying there. He had no knowledge of how Abraham, Indigo and Patch had saved so many lives. He stood up and looked over to the other side of the valley where Indigo and the American forces were. There was a silence, everyone was relieved to see the back of the Germans, but were saddened by the loss of their bridge.

Emmanuel asked the people now gathered if anyone had been on the bridge when it was blown up. A child turned to her and explained that a black man was standing firing a gun when the bridge was destroyed.

Everyone on both sides of the bridge had now worked out that Abraham Brown had saved countless lives with no consideration for his own.

Emmanuel's heart began to sink as all was told of this heroic act. She turned to Picard, François and Dominic and said, "Do you think there is any way he could have survived that?"

They all looked at her anxious face, each wondering why she seemed to care so much about him, and each shaking their head from side to side.

"I was wrong about these Yanks," stated Picard. "They were good men and truly are liberators of France."

Everybody agreed, and as time went on the crowd slowly dispersed, people making their way back to their homes in the village.

A big hole had made its presence known in Emmanuel's heart; besides the lovemaking they had both experienced she had seen a beautiful soulful being within him and wished for a miracle to happen.

When she got back to the farmhouse she went to her room, knelt by her bed and looked up at the wall where a crucifix hung, and prayed for Abraham's soul and for her sister. She knelt for a while, and before standing she reached under the bed for a pair of shoes. Her hands touched the chain of the dog tags belonging to Abraham, she raised them up and held them tightly in her hands, and then placed them in a box hidden under her bed in which she kept a few precious belongings that she felt an affinity with. She would keep them in remembrance of Abraham.

* * * * * *

Indigo and some of the American soldiers were now searching down in the valley for Abraham's body.

Unbeknown to everyone, Abraham had been blown off the bridge and projected into some large fir trees growing in the valley; the branches and foliage had absorbed the force of his body as it fell to earth at speed. His fall had been cushioned enough to give him a chance of survival and recovery.

Abraham lay beneath the tree that had saved his life. He was unconscious and had many injuries, including broken bones, his shirt being soaked in his own blood. Around him lay debris from the bridge, together with the remains of two of the American trucks which without the actions of Abraham would have been full of soldiers. Many other trucks crossing over the bridge would also have been lost without his heroism.

American soldiers were sent out into the valley to search for the German soldier who had detonated the explosives but no sign of him was found.

Abraham was discovered an hour after the bridge's destruction. Indigo rushed over to him as two medics attended to his wounds.

The thousand troops which made up the convoy were soon talking amongst themselves about what may have happened, were it not for Abraham and Indigo. When it became known that Abraham had survived, although critically wounded, every man prayed in his heart, or talked to fellow comrades all united in a hoped for common desire – this being for Abraham to somehow pull through the coma that he had now gone into and to survive and recover from his injuries.

Exaggerated stories soon developed of Abraham being some sort of superhuman, or born indestructible – this was far from the truth although in a spiritual way he was superhuman and now had insights far beyond the comprehension of mortal men.

Radio messages were now being sent out from the convoy to arrange urgent medical care for Abraham.

Indigo returned up to the road helping to stretcher Abraham out of the valley. The officer in charge of the convoy had explained everything to his superiors and a rescue aircraft was on its way to take Abraham to a mobile military hospital some fifty miles away. This special aeroplane could land and take off on a very short runway or farmer's field with short grass.

As Abraham was taken to a field next to the road where the truck convoy now waited, a large crowd of two hundred men had gathered to get a glimpse of him as they waited for the aeroplane to come in to land. The plane circled before descending and landed gently in a field of short grass. Abraham was stretchered over to the plane and secured aboard.

Indigo watched as the plane then taxied down to the bottom of the field, turned and prepared to take off into the wind. The engine opened up full throttle and away it went, the pilot steering the plane a short distance before enough lift could be obtained to get it airborne and away. As the plane ascended up into an empty sky a group of soldiers gathered around Indigo, one of them asking him questions. "Hey buddy, is it true that your friend saved hundreds of lives today by stopping the trucks crossing."

"Yes, that's true all right, and his name is Abraham Brown from Kentucky."

"I heard he's pretty badly hurt, do you think he's going to pull through?" said another soldier.

Indigo was careful not to say too much, as he would have sounded like a madman if he had told of Abraham's extraordinary abilities, so he decided just to answer any questions in a plain and simple way. "I hope he does pull though, he's a hero, many times over for his actions today," said Indigo.

The Sergeant stepped next to Indigo. "You're to come with me, Templeton, and make a full report before the convoy gets back on the road and makes its way to the next crossing."

This was fifteen miles away and in the opposite direction, giving the retreating Germans a good head start on their escape.

As Indigo walked back to a temporary command tent, hundreds of men were still gathered, and as Indigo walked towards them they parted down the middle. As he passed through he was cheered and patted on the back. This made him feel very proud as he made his way to the tent.

A farmer from Kentucky had saved so many that day and another had given his life – Patch Hancock, a hero and now at peace. His body was taken back to the village and laid out in an old abandoned church which was relatively undamaged by the war.

People started to feel different that day in the village with no name, and in everyone's heart it felt as if a curse had been lifted from them.

* * * * * *

Indigo made his report of the events of the last few days. He was now reunited with American forces and could carry out his duty and join them in ridding France of its evil invaders. The convoy would soon be mobile again and off to the next

133

river crossing. Indigo was given a rifle, helmet and some equipment. He felt very sad at the loss of Patch Hancock but knew that he would never forget him.

Indigo sat amongst his own countrymen and a big cheer went up as the truck convoy set off once more, each truck full of young men far, far from home. As Indigo rode in the truck the other soldiers fired questions at him in turn; when they all heard about Claus the Giant's part in the adventure together with two dogs, everyone was amazed and intrigued.

The convoy faded into the distance. The two tanks that had managed to cross over the bridge would meet the convoy at the next crossing in a few hours' time.

Messages were sent out from the village up to the monastery keeping them informed as to what had happened at the bridge.

Now people could relax, no longer living in constant fear of persecution, torture or death by the soldiers sent by Hitler to dominate the French. Today the village sprung back to life, the flowers opened and yielded their beauty like never before, the grassy fields seemed more lush than normal and people were mesmerised by the birdsongs which had not been heard for a very long time.

Today Picard, Emmanuel and the others would go to the monastery taking Claus with them, where he would be looked after for the time being. Emmanuel would visit her sister's grave and pay her respects.

Chapter Thirty-Five

As the plane descended to where the field hospital was sited, many people had gathered to catch a glimpse of Abraham. The plane lined up with the temporary runway and then dropped like a stone as it landed in a short space of time and distance. It taxied along to where two stretcher bearers stood ready. Whilst this was happening, even more people were gathering.

Abraham's seemingly lifeless body was taken into a large tent where medical staff awaited the VIP patient with anticipation. As he lay on the operating table he looked a mess; his shirt had been virtually torn to shreds by the blast. He was given a thorough examination which revealed that his left tibia and fibula were broken, together with his left wrist. He was then stripped naked and prepared for surgery.

Two very experienced surgeons who were familiar with severe injuries leant over him in preparation. "What's his pulse and breathing, Nurse Jennings?"

"I can't quite make it out, Doctor."

"What do you mean? Come on woman, hurry up!"

"Pulse appears to be once every ten seconds and breathing once every twenty seconds."

"Don't be ridiculous, woman! Let me listen." The surgeon placed his stethoscope over Abraham's slow heart rate to check out what the nurse had said. "You're right, Nurse Jennings, my apologies."

"What about his blood pressure?"

"I'm finding it difficult to get a proper reading, Doctor."

The doctor checked for himself and said, "That's far too low for someone to still be alive."

The other surgeon spoke. "Look, we have to operate now or he will die; God knows what internal injuries he has."

They immediately started operating to fix what they could.

As Abraham lay there, he started to dream one of a thousand dreams; these were no ordinary random dreams but guidelines to future events that one day would come Abraham's way in life. As he lay there, stories were now travelling about his heroic acts, and in the days ahead all America would know about him saving the lives of so many American soldiers, but not of his developing powers and insights – they were secret and only known to him and Indigo.

After the operation, Abraham was wheeled into a recovery ward for the evening and was kept separate from the other injured soldiers, not because he was black-skinned as was normally the case, but because he had become a hero and was, in a way, given celebrity status.

Everyone who came into contact with him would later tell others things like: "I touched him," or "I dressed his wounds." One nurse proudly boasted, "I have a piece of his shirt."

Deep within Abraham a force was at work, the usual healing process that cells undergo was being greatly accelerated. As he slept through the night the impossible was to happen medically speaking. No one could ever have imagined that the young Afro-American's injuries would almost disappear in one night.

* * * * * *

It was seven o'clock the next morning. Two excited nurses entered the room where Abraham lay.

"Clare, you take off any dressings that need changing and I'll check his blood pressure, pulse and breathing." The nurse leaned over Abraham and lifted his arm for the blood pressure reading. "He's got a kind face, don't you think Clare?"

"Yeah, I guess so," came the reply.

Both the nurses leaned over to look at his face a little closer.

"Yeah, he is kind and gentle looking you know."

Suddenly, totally unexpectedly, Abraham opened his eyes. Those big brown eyes examined both nurses, who were momentarily paralysed with disbelief. Abraham looked deeply into each of their eyes and they both saw something very different in this man. It was all too much for them, and as

Abraham started to sit himself up they ran out of the room screaming. Almost immediately, two armed soldiers together with a doctor entered the room.

"Where am I?" enquired Abraham.

The doctor and two guards just stood and looked at him in amazement – nobody had expected him to get through the night and live.

"Where am I, and why are you all staring at me like that?" repeated Abraham.

More doctors and medical staff entered the room, and one of the surgeons who had operated stepped forward. This was Captain Morehouse; he was tall and thin and wore a pair of spectacles halfway down his nose. He had deep set eyes and as he spoke his mouth would display his unhealthy and untidy looking teeth. "My dear Abraham, please lie back down before you do yourself a mischief," he exclaimed in a rather serious but confused manner.

The two armed guards left the room, which was now overcrowded with surgeons, doctors and nurses. Captain Morehouse talked amongst the other doctors for a while, discussing what to do about this unforeseen change of events, trying to make some sort of decision.

Abraham's shoulder felt warm, he knew now that he was safe, and remembered running over the bridge trying to get the children out of danger. "Hey!" he shouted. "Did those kids get off the bridge Ok? Did they?"

As Captain Morehouse was about to speak to him, into the room walked another two soldiers who firmly asked everyone to leave the room. "By whose authority?" asked Captain Morehouse.

"By my authority," replied a voice, as a Three Star General walked into the room; his name was General Conan. "Now get out of the room or I will have you put in the cells for the night."

He walked over to Abraham and waited whilst the room emptied of all the medical staff. Last to leave was Captain Morehouse, who gave the General a look of disgust and as he left muttered under his breath, "Who does he think he is?"

The General looked at Abraham and held out his hand. Abraham climbed out of bed and stood in front of him. The two men shook hands whilst a few more military personnel entered the room.

Abraham still felt a little shaky and asked for a glass of water and if he could sit down, to which the General replied "Sure. Do you know what you have done, Brown?" he asked.

"I'm not too sure, but hopefully I saved those children."

"Yes, you saved them all right, together with hundreds of American lives. You're a hero, Brown, and by all accounts you should be dead. But you're not, and people are saying that you have superhuman powers; is this true my boy?"

Abraham played it cool and just said that he had been lucky, and that maybe the doctors must have got it wrong about his injuries.

"Well, Brown, I have some questions for you later, but first I want you to let these people examine you. It's purely routine so don't worry about a thing."

A man holding written reports about the injuries that Abraham had sustained stepped forward as two other men started to examine him. They spoke in what sounded a strange way to Abraham's ear, but were merely using medical terminology.

As the examination continued, the two men looked on in amazement as they removed bandages and dressings to find the wounds almost completely healed. Another man took down their findings as the other people in the room looked on in awe at the medical dialogue and results.

A lot of noise was now coming from outside the giant hospital tent, as rumours were now spreading about what was going on, and the fact that a General had been flown in with persons unknown.

Even Abraham's broken bones had fused back together.

After Abraham had been fully examined, everyone except for General Conan left the room.

"Listen, Brown I am now going to be talking to people here and back in the US."

"But why?" enquired Abraham.

"Well, whatever you think about yourself or what has happened, the fact is that you are no ordinary man, and certain departments in the military and government need to know the facts."

"And then what, General?"

"I will come back in an hour and tell you my orders concerning you."

"Do I have a choice?"

"Not really."

"Can you tell me what happened to my friend Indigo?"

"I'll find out and tell you on my return." The General then left the room, and soon afterwards the two field hospital nurses came in and started to wash Abraham. Afterwards they supplied him with clean clothing and a small breakfast.

* * * * * *

Abraham became a little impatient as the hour that he had to wait seemed a lot longer. He was just about to get up and go and find the General himself, when in walked the very man. "Good news, Brown, your friend Indigo is fine and with a full division of men chasing the Germans across southern France."

"In that case, General, I should be with that division alongside Indigo. I'm a soldier, an American soldier."

"Hang on a minute," said the General, "you have nearly been blown to pieces, and fallen eighty feet to the ground, so you're not going anywhere until you're fighting fit."

"Ok, General, does that mean a week or maybe two?"

"Well, I have some new orders and they concern you. They are orders that even I was not expecting."

"What are they, what orders?"

"You are to be taken to Paris and then on to London."

"London! Is there a London in France?"

"No, Brown, I mean London, England."

"But, General, why, I don't understand?"

"All I know is that you have a lot of people interested in you and they want to find out what makes you tick."

"Who are they?"

"They are a secret war agency called Department S.P. It's an organisation made up of British, American and Allied personnel, very hush-hush."

Abraham did not want to hear such a thing as this.

"At midday you will be flown to Paris where you will stay overnight, to be briefed about your trip to England and taken to London the next day."

As Abraham was led out of the field hospital tent a large crowd awaited him again. They cheered and patted him on the back as he walked to the waiting aeroplane. It all felt very surreal, all this attention given by a white-skinned crowd to a solitary black man.

As he walked through the crowd, Abraham felt a slight limp. He thought to himself, "I am accepted because I have proved myself. I helped save white Americans so I am being treated differently than if I did not. Why can't all Afro-Americans just be accepted as ordinary people by white Americans?" The more he thought about it, the crazier it all seemed. Why should any black man have to prove himself before being accepted?

Abraham boarded the plane accompanied by the General and the men who had medically examined him. There was a strong side wind as the plane took off, making a smooth take-off difficult. Abraham did not like the sensation of being bounced around, this was the first flight he had made whilst conscious. He was not too keen on this new experience of flying.

Not a lot was said on the two hour flight, and as the plane circled in to land, Abraham's breath was taken away by the view he saw below.

"What's that tall structure down there?" he asked.

The General laughed and replied, "That's the Eiffel Tower; it's a thousand feet high I think. Have you never seen a picture of it before Brown?"

"No, I don't think so," answered Abraham. "What's it for and why was it built?"

"You'd better ask a Parisian about that, 'cos I'm damned if I know."

Chapter Thirty-Six

Back home in America, stories were now starting to spread like wildfire about the actions of Abraham at the bridge, saving so many lives. Indigo was also being talked about together with the unfortunate death of Patch Hancock. Cars were despatched to each of their homes, taking the news of the three men's heroic deed. Each car had a driver and two passengers, one a military representative and the other a government representative.

As one of the cars approached the house where Mrs Hancock was just finishing off some housework, eyes were watching as the grey car cruised slowly down the street. People became curious and stepped outside to follow the car. It stopped outside the house, the driver just sitting still and looking straight ahead as the two passengers stepped out from either side of the vehicle. Both men then stood side by side and walked together up the path to the front door. As the bell rang inside, Patch's mother was just about to sit down. "Dammit, who's that now?" she thought to herself. She approached the front door and could see the silhouette of the two men through the frosted glass. They looked rather serious, official looking men. She opened the door and stood face to face with them.

"Mrs Hancock?" said one of the men.

"Yes, and who wants to know?" came the reply.

"Can we come in, please, we have some news concerning your son, Scott."

Her heart sank and her legs turned to jelly as she now realised what was about to happen.

The two men helped her to a chair and the front door was closed.

Ten minutes passed and the door opened again. The two men walked out, pulling the door shut behind them.

Neighbours had gathered at the gate, curious about what was going on. The two men walked through the small crowd and got back into the car. It drove to the end of the street, took a turn left and was gone.

Two women approached the house to see if they could comfort the mother inside, who now cried a thousand tears at the loss of her only son. The two women had guessed what had happened.

* * * * * *

Another car was at the home of Mr and Mrs Templeton. This car only had one passenger who gave them the news that their son was a hero, and as he explained to Indigo's mother and father the events leading up the bridge's destruction, they felt so very proud of their son. They were both committed Christians and in their hearts they rejoiced that the son they had been blessed with and had brought into the world together, had saved so many lives, sparing all the relatives of those men so much pain and anguish.

When the car drove off, they both cried tears of joy and prayed for Indigo to survive the rest of the war and return home.

Indigo's father knew of his son's gambling debts, and before this day had felt a little bitter in his heart about it, but now all that melted away to become a fleeting memory.

Mr and Mrs Templeton ran out into the street and embraced everyone they met, they ran through the neighbourhood singing, laughing and shouting for all to hear.

* * * * * *

Abraham's mother was helping in the lower corner of the field nearest the house. She and Abraham's siblings could see a car approaching. Mrs Brown told them both to go to the house and stay inside until she told them otherwise. The car pulled up and two men clambered out. The ground was dusty and dry and as they walked to where Mrs Brown was standing they felt exposed and uncomfortable.

"Mrs Brown?" enquired one of the men.

"Yes, I am Mrs Brown, what can I do for you two gentlemen?"

"Well, Mrs Brown, would you prefer to talk in the house? We have some news about your son, Abraham."

"Oh!" replied Mrs Brown, her heart sinking a little as she braced herself for bad news. "I am fine standing here, thank you. Please go ahead and tell me what news you have of my son."

"Don't fret, please, madam, we bring good news about him, very good news indeed."

Abraham's mother looked mystified and was now very curious "Go on!" she demanded. "What news of Abraham do you have?"

"He is a hero, and has saved many lives in southern France." The men then continued in detail about the events at the bridge. "As we speak, preparations are under way to take Abraham to London, England."

"London, England!" she exclaimed.

"Yes, Mrs Brown, your son will be helping with some secret research projects that both our American scientists and the British scientists are now working on to try and bring this war to a swift end."

"What sort of research projects?"

"I'm afraid that information is classified and we even don't know ourselves, Mrs Brown."

She thought for a moment and then said, "Well, I guess he's safer in London than fighting the Germans isn't he?"

She looked at the two men expecting a very positive response, but all they could do was force a smile and nod their heads approvingly at her.

The two men left the house and were driven off into the distance.

Mrs Brown shouted out to her son and daughter waiting in the house.

"Come out, you two! Abraham is a hero and is going to London, England for a while."

Mrs Brown then explained all about the heroism of their brother, Abraham.

Chapter Thirty-Seven

As the plane took off from Paris, Abraham looked down on the city, remembering his passionate time with Emmanuel, "I hope she is all right," he thought to himself. His mind was still somewhat muddled due to his injuries and his body still ached a little.

The plane was a Dakota with only a few passengers on board. Abraham felt a little uncomfortable amongst the white passengers and the mixture of American and English accents.

"Hey, Abraham Brown," said a voice in a rather sceptical and discerning way. "Is it true that you have incredible powers and that you can even cheat death?"

Abraham looked up at the man and made sure he made eye contact with him before giving his reply. As their eyes lined up visually, the man stepped back a pace.

"I am what I am, a black man, a farmer, an American, and lucky to be alive by all accounts, but not superhuman, no. That's just for the comic books. People will think and say what they want. It's as simple as that."

"Why, then, are you on this plane like the rest of us, and why are you going to Department S.P. in London?"

"I have no idea, but as far as I am concerned they are wasting their time, and I will soon prove this to them."

"And then what, Abraham Brown?"

"I will ask to be sent back to France to join the Allied forces in driving the Germans out."

Abraham's eyes were now intensely focused on the other man's eyes, and he realised that if he wanted to he could somehow hurt the man, so he looked away and refused to answer any more questions about himself.

As the flight continued, an attractive, slim and unassuming woman came and sat beside him; her name was Miss Armstrong. She had been seconded to Department S.P. from Military Intelligence.

"Hello, Mr Brown," she said, in a voice and accent that Abraham had not encountered in a woman before. "My name is Miss Armstrong and I will be your chaperone whilst you are with Department S.P."

"What's this all about, lady?" came his reply as he turned and looked straight at her. He was a bit wound up, but as he looked at her his shoulder warmed and tingled a little. This made him realise she was not like the over inquisitive man earlier in the flight. She had an aura about her and as they briefly talked, he felt more and more comfortable in her presence. Her eyes were blue and twinkled as she spoke. She was a woman who always wore a smile whatever the time, place or situation. She was a brunette, but her uniform and hat hid most of her natural beauty.

The Dakota passed over the English coastline and was soon ready to land at an airfield twenty miles from the centre of London. The plane circled and made its descent to the runway. It taxied towards a large hangar before coming to a halt.

Abraham and the other passengers made their way off the plane; they were escorted into the hangar by an armed guard of eight men. Once inside they were asked a few questions and shortly afterwards were sitting on a coach headed for a secret location in London.

Abraham watched with interest, the landscape and buildings en route to Department S.P. He noticed especially how things looked on a smaller scale than back home. The roads and cars seemed so much smaller and the roads turned and twisted as they travelled the first few miles from the airfield. The coach seemed pretty cramped too. He turned to Miss Armstrong who sat on the opposite side of the coach and asked, "Have you run out of things like metal in this country?"

"No, why do you ask, Abraham?"

"Well, Miss, the cars I see on the roads here, have they been made smaller for any reason?"

"No, Abraham, they are quite normal automobiles as you Americans like to call them."

"Then are you British mainly small in stature?" he asked.

"No, Abraham, I think you will find things very similar to America, but at the same time very different."

"Different, but how?"

"Well, as you have observed the cars are smaller, but if you break down what they are made from and how they are manufactured then it is the same."

"Oh, I kinda see, and I've noticed that even your houses are much smaller."

"You'll get used to it, Abraham."

"I guess so."

"How are you feeling now?" said a voice from a few seats behind.

Abraham turned around and answered the man who had spoken. "Oh, I feel fine, but I still think that this is one big waste of time as far as I'm concerned."

"Well, please be patient and give it a few days with Department S.P."

"Maybe."

As Abraham sat and closed his eyes, he realised for the first time that his dog tags were missing and he had no idea what had happened to them or where they could be, "Miss Armstrong."

"Yes, Abraham, what can I do for you?"

"Well, Miss, it would appear my dog tags are missing and may be lost. Can you arrange for some new replacement ones for me?"

"Certainly, Abraham, leave it with me."

Abraham sat and once more looked out of the window, making mental notes on how England was so very different from back home in Kentucky.

* * * * * *

As the coach entered London, the reality of war was once more apparent to Abraham as he observed buildings destroyed by German bombing raids.

Everything seemed to be in slow motion for a while as he tried to comprehend the desolation that he was now witnessing. As they travelled through one area, whole rows of houses were now mere brick carcases, and everything within them destroyed either by the bombs' explosive forces or the fires that raged after the bombing raids; infernos consuming everything until they became ash, house and human.

"Miss Armstrong?" asked Abraham.

"Yes, Abraham, is everything all right?"

"Is all London like this?"

"Like what, exactly?"

"Well, all smashed up and burnt."

"Yes, a lot of London is like this, but not everywhere," she added.

"How can the Germans do this to civilians, Miss Armstrong?" Abraham could not believe what he was seeing.

"I'm afraid that we do the same to the German towns and cities."

"What? Surely not, that's inhuman! I mean, war is war but that is pure evil. Who started it? Someone must have started this madness."

"I don't know, Abraham," came Miss Armstrong's reply. She was a little embarrassed by his question and felt a little ashamed at the fact that as far as bombings were concerned, the British appeared to be as bad as the Germans. "We're nearly there now, Abraham."

He and the other passengers were instructed to fix their eyes on the floor as they were nearing their secret destination. The coach travelled down a narrow side street in Greenwich, and then turned into a cobbled yard passing under an arched sign which spanned the pillared entranceway. The sign read "Smith's Distillery" which was purely a smokescreen, as this was the entranceway to Department S.P.

The large iron gates closed automatically. No sooner had this happened than another set of smaller timber double doors opened and the coach drove in. The driver turned off the engine and left the coach.

"What next?" thought Abraham to himself.

The coach was parked in an old warehouse. Several lights came on, illuminating the large storage area in a brighter than normal light. The passengers started to get off the coach, leaving Abraham and Miss Armstrong to the end.

"Come on, Abraham, don't be shy."

Abraham stood up and made his way to the door, where he paused for a moment and then stepped off the coach, followed by Miss Armstrong.

Everyone's attention was drawn to a short, oriental looking man wearing round spectacles, his shoes tapping as he walked straight towards the awaiting guests. "Good morning, ladies and gentlemen, my name is Dr Chen. I am the lead scientist here, please follow me to the dining room where refreshments, or if you prefer, a hot meal, awaits you."

Miss Armstrong turned to Abraham and said, "I have to carry on with my other duties now, Abraham, but will see you in a day or two after you have settled in. Goodbye for now." She walked over to another part of the warehouse and disappeared through a brown door.

Abraham still felt a little uncomfortable, as he did not know anyone else or understand how he would be able to help these well-educated and scientific types that he now found himself amongst.

* * * * * *

Soon, all the passengers from the coach were sitting at a big table, happily eating and drinking as they observed each other and their new and alien surroundings. There were other people in the dining room, but they took no noticeable interest in the new arrivals.

Dr Chen walked around the table and placed a plain coloured card in front of each person then said, "When we descend in the elevator to the research facility, you must each keep your card and note that you are only allowed to enter rooms that have doors of the same colour."

"What if we forget or make an error?" enquired a voice.

"That I cannot answer, because as long as you do what is expected of you, I will be in charge of your visit, but any violation or breaking of the rules will result in you being handed to the Military Commander here. I have heard he can be a right bastard if he wants to, be so please just enjoy your stay and do what is asked of you."

When everyone had finished eating Dr Chen escorted them down to the underground facility. Here, they were shown their accommodation and each introduced to a scientist with whom they would be working over the next few days, to try and enhance their skills and abilities in certain fields of scientific war research and redevelopment.

"Ah, Mr Brown, you will be assisting me in my work," said Dr Chen.

"And what would that be, Doctor?" replied Abraham.

"We believe that certain things in life can be predicted or foreseen by certain people. We are also interested in your body's reaction to injury and what seems to be an accelerated healing ability possessed by you, Abraham."

"Oh, I see. What will happen then?"

"We will make a report, and you may be asked to join us in developing new ways to defeat the Germans."

"Do you mean making new weapons?" asked Abraham.

"If that is required, then yes."

"I have a problem with that, Dr Chen, as to what is to stop such weapons being used on civilian populations."

"Sometimes we have to make such decisions and must choose the lesser of two evils."

"Are the Nazis as evil and as big a threat as people are saying?"

"Yes, Abraham, and I can assure you that we have to stop them whatever the cost."

"But surely their armies are on the retreat now?"

"Yes, Abraham, but we have been getting reports that soon we will face a new and deadly weapon here in this great city, one that we will have no warning of or way of stopping," replied Dr Chen.

* * * * * *

Abraham spent a while being briefed by Dr Chen and was given some books to read at his leisure that night.

That evening he looked over the books and became most interested in many of the things the books contained.

Abraham's room was very basic and contained a bunk bed, a table and two chairs, a small washbasin but no toilet facilities. For these a trip down the corridor was required if one needed to relieve oneself. There was a very basic pendant light that hung in the middle of the room, and every so often the bulb would flicker, stop and then work again for at least half an hour.

Abraham made a few notes with the pen and paper that lay on the table top. As his eyes tired, he decided to call it a day and washed his face in the sink. He opened a small cabinet on the wall which contained soaps for washing and shaving together with a few razor blades. He decided to shave and removed his shirt. As he stood in front of the sink and began to shave, the light flickered once more; he remembered back to when Emmanuel had stood naked behind him in her room only a few days ago in the French farmhouse. His shoulder warmed and tingled with these thoughts, telling him it was a good thing that had happened that day with Emmanuel.

The room had no windows as it was subterranean, and Abraham could feel a change in the normal air pressure.

As he lay in bed with the light off and in total darkness, a few footsteps in the corridor would now and then pass the room; a small line of dim light emanated from beneath the door as he gently drifted to sleep.

Chapter Thirty-Eight

Life in France was getting back to normal at the monastery and in the village with no name.

Claus the Giant had been taken in by the brothers, his mind still as that of a child. His tongue had started to heal but he still could not speak properly. His two dogs, Death and Destruction, never returned and by now must have now found a new master and home.

Freddie Richards's stay was nearing an end and arrangements for him to return to England were being made. He would return to his Spitfire squadron based at Exeter in Devon.

In the village, next to the useless and damaged bridge, repairs were now well under way. Even the village was beginning to become more like a normal one, and the terrible atmosphere that had surrounded it for so long had now lifted. Life seemed easier for people now, not living in fear but free to be as they should be.

At the farmhouse Emmanuel had acquired some new cows and chickens. She lay in bed each evening and prayed in her heart that maybe one day she would meet another man like Abraham, who would treat her well and they could live happily together. She craved the tenderness that she had always been denied by men but had now found in Abraham. Her cousin Picard had decided to help her get the farm running smoothly before doing anything else with his life.

France had been finally freed from its soulless invaders who had been driven out, leaving so much desolation behind them. Now the grace and beauty of this land could start to be restored by the ever resilient French people.

* * * * * *

Back in America, the media used the saving of lives at the bridge for propaganda, mainly referring to Patch Hancock and Indigo Templeton, although it was largely Abraham Brown's actions that led to so many young lives being saved. Racism had changed the reality of the facts and events, portraying him as a minor part in the story. Even Mrs Hancock and Mr and Mrs Templeton were never given the full facts about the heroism of the young farmer from Kentucky.

* * * * * *

As Abraham slept beneath the mighty and scarred city of London he had a new set of dreams, one concerning Miss Armstrong and the other, Dr Chen.

Department S.P. were working with people who were reputed to have Extra Sensory Perception, or ESP. Abraham was similar to such people, but he could never see or predict the future, his dreams only revealed secrets of the present and the past. He would, out of principle, be unwilling to co-operate with anyone who would use his knowledge or abilities in the name of violence or aggression. Although a young man of twenty-five, and not too sure about his own religious beliefs, Abraham had been brought up a Christian and knew that the values it had taught him were right and true. He often wondered why even white folks who went to church every Sunday still treated the coloured community of any race as second class citizens.

* * * * * *

As Abraham slept safely underground, the Germans were planning to use a new weapon, and London was to be one of its new targets; a weapon that could not be detected or stopped, a weapon with the potential to destroy whole towns and cities should their numbers be enough.

This weapon was a rocket called the V2.

The V1 had been menacing enough, striking fear into every man, woman and child as its evil sounding engine droned through the skies, and then nothing as the ramjet engine would without warning stop, leaving the giant flying bomb to plummet downwards, its massive explosive payload ready to kill the innocent population beneath, wreaking death and destruction like as never seen before in the modern world. The Germans now possessed the technology to strike even more terror onto London, their ability to advance jet engine technology being way above all others making these new weapons, which seemed almost unbelievable. Science fiction had now evolved into science fact.

The jet engine had first been developed around the same time by both Britain and Germany. It had now been advanced beyond anyone's dreams by the insane drive of Nazi Germany.

The V2s were now just a few days from their launch on London. This weapon would be the first man-made object in the history of the world to enter outer space. A weapon that once over its target would plummet to earth at supersonic speed, breaking the sound barrier many times over on its trajectory of death.

Department S.P. knew of this new weapon, but had no idea of the impending launch on the city that stood above them.

Chapter Thirty-Nine

It was seven o'clock the next morning, and a wall mounted loudspeaker opposite to where Abraham slept, sprang into life. Its message was also being piped into all the other rooms where the new arrivals had spent their first night.

"Please assemble for breakfast at eight o'clock – do not forget your coloured card which shows your permitted areas of access."

Abraham washed and dressed quickly, he made his way to the toilet at the end of the corridor and then made his way to the dining room where everyone was assembling.

As everyone had met briefly the previous day the atmosphere seemed more relaxed, and as Abraham looked around whilst eating his food, he noticed that the people there were mainly men together with a few women. What surprised him most was that he wasn't the only dark skinned person there. This seemed very unusual and his curiosity was aroused.

He looked up as Dr Chen entered the room. He had another ten people with him, all dressed in white coats and each carrying an attaché case, the contents being relevant to each of their fields of expertise.

Armed guards were standing in each corner of the room, but they did not look at all menacing or intimidating. They remained inconspicuous, blending into the background.

People started to be selected by Dr Chen's colleagues. Names were called and the people put into groups.

Abraham was the last one left at the table. As everyone else in the room filed away, Dr Chen approached him and spoke. "Good Morning, Abraham."

"Good Morning, Dr Chen."

"You're with me today, Abraham, you ready to make a start?"

"Sure, that's OK with me." Abraham stood up and followed Dr Chen along a few corridors, each having a different coloured door.

They stopped outside a green door. "What's your colour, Abraham?" asked Dr Chen.

"My colour?" came the reply.

"Yes, the card you were given, what colour is it?"

"Oh, that colour. It's green, Dr Chen."

"Then this is our room today young man, come on in."

They entered the dimly lit room, it was very large and in the centre stood what looked like a giant egg box.

"Now, Abraham, I would like you to do a few simple tests this morning."

"What sort of tests, Doctor?"

"You will be enclosed in that strange looking capsule in the middle of the room."

"That's a capsule?" exclaimed Abraham.

"Yes, it's a special structure for the type of tests we will be doing."

Abraham's curiosity was whetted, which made him ask "Why is it that strange shape?"

"Once you are securely inside I will speak to you via a microphone and give you instructions."

"OK, Doctor, but why is that shape?" he repeated.

"It's been specially designed to keep out any interference such as noise, radio waves, heat, cold, vibration and so on – nothing can enter or leave the capsule."

Dr Chen opened the strange looking contraption and made sure that Abraham was comfortable and secure before closing it. He walked over to a desk where he sat down and made preparations to start.

"Can you hear me, Abraham?"

"Yes, Dr Chen, I hear you OK."

"Then I will begin. I'm looking at some cards which have pictures and numbers on. Tell me if you can pick up what I am seeing."

Abraham sat in the darkness of the capsule; he concentrated as much as possible but could not make out any of the images.

"Can you see what I am looking at, Abraham?"

"No, Doctor Chen, I see nothing and I don't have the ability you are looking for in me."

"Mmm, I see. Abraham, do you believe in such an ability in humans?"

"Not really, Doctor Chen, all I know is that I have a gift. It is of a different kind from what this Department is interested in."

"So you can heal very quickly and see things in dreams that give you explanations?"

"Yes, Doctor Chen, that is what I have been telling people ever since I was skewered by a Nazi bayonet last week."

"Do you believe in mind reading, Abraham?"

"Not really."

"But you accept your own developing and new found abilities don't you?"

"Yes, Doctor Chen, but I never asked or wished for any of this."

"What if I said I could prove to you that ESP really exists?"

"Well, you would have to show me first and demonstrate, then I may go along with it."

"In that case, Abraham, let's try an experiment. I want you to think about something fresh in your mind and I will give you my interpretation of what it is."

As Abraham started to open his mind, his left shoulder became painful as he remembered a dream from only hours before in which he had seen an image of Doctor Chen, an image in which men dressed as Nazis were speaking with him, all sitting round a giant table inside a magnificent looking building adorned with swastikas. There was a deadly silence as Abraham recalled the dream and realised that it meant something, together with the now increasing pain in his left shoulder.

The silence continued and was eventually broken by Doctor Chen's voice. "Are you still concentrating, Abraham?"

"Yes, Doctor Chen," came the reply.

A game of cat and mouse then ensued between the two men.

Could Doctor Chen see Abraham's dream, and if so, what could it mean?

Chapter Forty

"Abraham, I have to get some more documents before we finish. I will only be a few minutes."

"Then please let me out of here Doctor Chen, as it is a bit claustrophobic in here."

"I will not be long." Doctor Chen left the room, his footsteps tip tapping along as he went.

All Abraham could do was listen, as Doctor Chen had left the microphone switched on.

Abraham was now in trouble; big, big trouble. He knew that Doctor Chen had seen his dream somehow. His shoulder pains were now telling him of impending danger. He started to sweat, his breathing increasing. He was just about to go into a mild panic when he heard the door open in the room outside the capsule. It closed gently. He began to think something bad was about to happen when he realised that the footsteps sounded different – quieter, softer – then they stopped.

"Hey, get me out of here, get me out, whoever you are, get me out!"

Silence was the reply.

A few moments passed and the door to the room opened again.

"Don't go!" shouted Abraham.

Then to Abraham's dismay, the door shut closed and once more the tip tap of Doctor Chen's shoes echoed into the microphone for Abraham to hear.

He sat, not knowing why Doctor Chen had left the room or what was going to happen next.

"Abraham, I am going to open the capsule so please do not make any sudden moves or try anything silly, as I now have a pistol in my right hand and I will not hesitate to use it."

Abraham remained silent, he now became very calm as Doctor Chen opened the capsule.

"OK, Abraham, out you come, nice and easy please."

Doctor Chen and Abraham stood in front of the capsule, the room still very dimly lit.

"What should I do with you, Abraham Brown eh?"

"Let me go would be nice. Just let me leave the room."

"That I would like to do, but your dream has portrayed me as a Nazi collaborator, is that not true?"

"Yes, I guess so, Doctor."

"Then I have no choice but to shoot you here and now." Doctor Chen produced a silencer from his coat pocket and attached it to the barrel of his pistol.

* * * * * *

Doctor Chen was an eminent Chinese scientist whose family had been kidnapped by the Japanese and held captive – his whole family, immediate and distant, not just his wife and two children but his mother, father, sisters and brothers with their families.

He had been taken to Berlin by the Japanese and forced by the Nazis to spy for them, as they knew of the formation of a new secret department based underground somewhere in London. At first he refused, but as the list of hostages grew, he gave in to the Nazis' evil scheme. All he had to do was to inform them of the activities of Department S.P. This would help the Nazis stay one step ahead of the new technologies and weapons now being developed by the Allies.

He was taken back to China and eventually recruited to Department S.P. by the British, who had been following his work in Extra Sensory Perception for several years beforehand. Together with a network of spies and informers working in London, this was exactly what the Nazis had anticipated.

* * * * * *

"Is there no other way out of this situation, Doctor Chen?"

"I can do one of three things here, Abraham Brown – I can shoot you, I can shoot myself or I can hand myself in."

Silence ensued as Abraham's eyes met Doctor Chen's in a look never seen or felt by Chen before.

He saw a deep power within Abraham, one that would only be used for good. Now he had second thoughts about shooting him, but in his mind's eye could see his family held captive, only to be killed if he did not continue to pass secrets on to the Nazis.

The gun was still pointed at Abraham, but he felt no danger now and a light tingle came from his shoulder. What on earth could save him from the impending bullet which was now being selected, as the semi-automatic pistol was being primed? The corners of the room were in total darkness because of the special low light within it. From one of the corners facing Doctor Chen's left-hand side, an arm emerged into the low light, and in the hand of the outstretched arm, held tightly and steadily, was a British Service revolver. A female finger was wrapped around the trigger, primed and ready to shoot without mercy or a second thought. "Put the gun down, Doctor Chen," said a female voice.

Slowly, Chen's head turned and said, "You know I cannot do that."

Abraham had recognised the female voice as that of Miss Armstrong.

"Then I will do my duty, Doctor Chen."

"You British seem to think it is your God given right to do your duty for King and country, but you are merely clinging to the attitude indoctrinated into you by trying to keep the British Empire alive."

"Drop your gun, Doctor Chen, please drop it!" Abraham implored.

"It seems there is only one way out of this now, Abraham." As Doctor Chen spoke, Miss Armstrong stepped out of the shadows. Doctor Chen dropped the gun on to the floor, took off his spectacles and reached into his coat pocket.

"My gun is still pointing at you, Doctor Chen, so don't try anything stupid."

"My dear girl, I am merely putting away my spectacles, that is all."

Abraham felt relieved, but his shoulder still ached and he didn't quite know what was about to happen. He knew that things were not quite over yet.

As Doctor Chen opened the case and placed his spectacles inside, neither Abraham nor Miss Armstrong had noticed his sleight of hand, as he took out two cyanide capsules from within the case. He placed the case back into his pocket and then made out he was coughing. As he did so he raised his hand to his mouth and quickly placed the capsules into it. He bit down hard and swallowed several times, sending the liquid death down into his body. The Nazis had given the capsules to him in the event of his activities ever being discovered. He was told that if he did not do this and remained alive or in detention, then his family would face certain death, a slow and painful death at that. This thought had now raced through Chen's tortured mind as he would now never see the family he loved so dearly again.

Doctor Chen fell to his knees, his face reacting to the excruciating pain he was experiencing.

Abraham knelt down next to him and asked, "Why, Doctor Chen, why?"

Chen crumpled into a twisted heap of human composition. Miss Armstrong re-holstered her revolver and walked over to where they were. Abraham stood up and together they both looked down at Chen.

"What has just happened, Miss Armstrong, and why?" asked Abraham.

"I will explain everything to you later," she replied.

"How did he kill himself then?"

"It seems he took poison."

"Poison? What sort of poison does that to a man?"

Abraham had been quite shocked by everything that had happened, and did not know that Doctor Chen's laboratory had been bugged and that Miss Armstrong, together with other Intelligence Officers, knew that there was a spy in the organisation. They had used Abraham as a lure.

Doctor Chen claimed he had the ability to read minds and they hoped he would see something in Abraham's mind that would spook him, and in this case it did.

Miss Armstrong had entered the room whilst Chen had gone to get his gun. She had hidden in one of the corners which were in total darkness and stood behind a medical examinations screen using this as further cover.

Doctor Chen had died using the preferred and adopted way of the Third Reich.

The cyanide was prussic acid, in liquid form, nasty stuff that would eat through a man's insides. In this case it worked extremely quickly as Doctor Chen had not eaten at breakfast, his body being an empty vessel for the poison to penetrate easily into. He had also taken two capsules to ensure a quick and guaranteed death.

The twenty-eight members of his family were never seen or heard of again – the Japanese could be as evil as any Nazi.

Chapter Forty-One

The door opened and two military policemen together with an intelligence officer entered the room.

"You OK, Miss Armstrong?" asked the intelligence officer.

"Yes, I'm fine."

"And you, Mr Brown, are you OK?"

"I will be when someone explains what all his has been about."

"Any questions will be answered later. Miss Armstrong will be taking you to a de-briefing meeting at four o'clock, so until then I suggest you go and enjoy the sights of London."

"You mean, I can go up above ground and walk about?" said Abraham in surprise.

"Yes, but don't leave Miss Armstrong's side."

"That's fine by me," answered Abraham in an excited voice.

"Come with me, Abraham, I have something for you," said Miss Armstrong.

She took him to the main Control Room within Department S.P. whilst the two military policemen took Chen's twisted corpse to an army mortuary a few miles away.

Abraham followed Miss Armstrong through what seemed a never ending labyrinth of corridors. Eventually, they came to a set of double doors; an armed guard stood on either side. Miss Armstrong opened both doors and stepped inside with Abraham next to her. As they both filed in, everyone in the gigantic looking room turned and clapped before returning to their duties.

Miss Armstrong led Abraham to a table situated just inside the room, and to the right, on the table were two boxes, one large, the other small.

"They are for you, Abraham," said Miss Armstrong.

"For me, are you sure?"

"Yes," she replied with a chuckle. "Go on, open them."

Abraham reached out and picked up the smaller box. He lifted the lid and there, to his surprise, lay a brand new set of dog tags. A big smile spanned his face as he put them over his head to hang down in front of his chest. "Why, thank you Miss Armstrong."

He reached over and lifted the lid of the larger box sitting on the table. It contained a brand new uniform; this one had been tailor made for him using fabrics that were of the very best quality. "Whoa!" gasped Abraham.

"Well?" asked Miss Armstrong. "What do you think?"

"Very nice, Miss, very nice indeed," Abraham's happy go lucky smile showing how he felt.

He was shown to a room where he could change and freshen up. After a while he emerged back into the main Control Room. He looked a most handsome fellow and Miss Armstrong, for some reason best known only to herself, smiled and gave him a cheeky wink of her eye.

"Come on Abraham, we have to be upstairs in five minutes as our ride will be waiting."

* * * * * *

The army jeep pulled out of the outer distillery doors into Brewers Mews and headed for the centre of London. As the jeep weaved its way around Westminster, Abraham was dumbstruck by buildings he had never seen or could ever have imagined before. "These are mighty grand buildings, Miss Armstrong," he said with astonishment in his voice.

The jeep travelled on and passed Buckingham Palace, where it slowed down to a crawl.

"Who lives here?" he enquired.

"This is where the King lives when he is in London."

"Wow! What's it like having a King, Miss Armstrong?"

"I like it, but there are some that don't, and if your fellow Americans had not gained independence from us British in 1776 he would be your king as well."

"What's his name?"

"He's called King George VI, and it was another George who was king when your country gained independence from us."

"That's my younger brother's name, but he ain't got any numbers after it, just plain old George Brown."

The jeep travelled all around central London. To a farmer from Kentucky it was like being on another planet, except here everyone spoke English as he did.

The jeep stopped by Tower Bridge where Miss Armstrong got out and said, "Come on, Abraham, we're going back to Greenwich by boat."

"See you in a while, Miss Armstrong," said the jeep driver, before he drove over Tower Bridge and headed eastwards back to Greenwich.

"That's a fancy looking bridge," commented Abraham as he and Miss Armstrong walked to some steps by the side of the River Thames where a naval launch was waiting for them. They were helped aboard, and away the small craft went. As it made its way downstream towards the East End, Abraham took one final look behind him and marvelled at all the sights he had seen. He knew nothing about the British or their lives, but was enjoying himself and becoming more familiar with this alien environment and its people. He turned to Miss Armstrong and asked, "If the Germans ever reach London what do you think they will do?"

"To the city or to the people?"

"Both, I guess."

She thought for a moment and then replied, "I think they would leave London as it is, but as for the people then I dread to think what their fate would be. What makes men so evil, Abraham?"

"Fear, ignorance, suspicion, all the traits that keep holding us back in life."

"Yes, I suppose you have a point there, Abraham. Let's hope that after this terrible war, nations will look back at it and never take up arms against one another again."

The boat slowed down as it reached a jetty where the MP and the driver of the jeep stood waiting. They tied up the mooring ropes and helped Miss Armstrong and Abraham ashore.

"It's three forty-five, Miss Armstrong," said the driver.

To which she replied, "Oh, yes, we'd better not be late had we!"

As the jeep made its way through Greenwich, Abraham was asked to look at the floor, as Department S.P. Headquarters were meant to be secret, but because Abraham had proved his worth twice now, nobody in the jeep bothered to look and see if he was obeying the instruction.

The streets became smaller as the jeep travelled along, before turning into Brewers Mews and finally through the gates at Smith's Distillery. The usual etiquette and procedures were observed as they entered the building and went down into the depths beneath the mighty city.

As they made their way to the Control Room to be briefed, Abraham asked Miss Armstrong a question. "I notice that the people have such a variety of skin colour and features. Is there a reason for that as I have never before in my life seen so many races working together in one building?"

"Ah, I see," said Miss Armstrong. "Well, it's really very simple. As you know the British once had a mighty empire and now the war is being fought, many of those countries fight together with us as allies in defeating the Nazis."

"How many men?" asked Abraham.

"Tens of thousands of brave young men like yourself." She continued, "All these countries stand together with us in stopping the Germans and Japanese. These allies have sent their top scientists here from their respective countries to come up with new weapons, medicines, ideas, anything that can help to defeat Mr Hitler and his madness."

"What about Doctor Chen?"

"It's like this. Doctor Chen was keeping the Germans informed of all our secret projects – hence the name Department S.P. – so every time we thought we were advancing forward and beyond the Germans, we were instantly betrayed by him."

"Oh, I see, but why did he do it, did he hate the free world that much?"

"No, Abraham, he had no choice as it would appear his family were being held hostage by the Japanese who were under instruction by Berlin."

Abraham thought back to when he first met Doctor Chen. His shoulder did not ache or hurt which would have told him Chen was an evil man. It would appear he was a decent sort but had no choice but to do as the Nazis ordered him, or every relative he had would die. What a choice!

Abraham was led to the Control Room, where the doors were already being held open by a military policeman on either side. He and Miss Armstrong walked in, his eyes surveying the environment as they entered. The room looked even bigger than before, the ceiling was arched and built of brick construction. A giant table stood centrally in the room and was now surrounded by many high ranking military and civilian personnel. People were smoking and holding glasses in their hands as they chatted amongst one another. The room was very smoky, which made Abraham wish he could open a window.

As they both stood there, the room suddenly became silent as everyone's attention was drawn to the presence of Abraham. Everyone in the room formed two lines between Abraham and the table. Miss Armstrong stood to one side, as a serious looking, portly man smoking a giant cigar approached Abraham. The two men each surveyed the other, Abraham looking very smart in his new uniform.

The man then spoke in a very direct and powerful sounding voice. "Good afternoon, Mr Brown."

Everyone looked on in silence, almost afraid to breathe.

"Good afternoon, sir," came Abraham's reply.

"We are deeply indebted to you, Abraham Brown, as you have helped to expose an informer and traitor in our organisation." The man spoke with such command and authority it was obvious to Abraham that he was no ordinary man, but a powerful man, a leader of men and a nation.

The man held out his hand, and he and Abraham shook hands. Abraham sensed the devotion, drive and duty which emanated from this man. He now knew this could only be one person; he had heard of him many times but had never seen a photograph.

The man leading the British against the tyranny of Hitler and his henchmen now stood here, staring Abraham right in the face.

Everyone in the room still looked on in silence.

"Do you know who I am, young man?"

Abraham smiled and said, "Yes, sir, you are Mr Winston Churchill, I think."

"You think, you think?" came the reply.

Everyone was aghast until a moment later the man burst out into rapturous laughter.

A sigh of relief swept around the room as all joined in with their leader's response.

"Yes, you are correct, I am Winston Churchill, and I would like you to stay here with Department S.P. for a week and work on some projects which are being investigated and developed by all these good people from the far corners of the world."

Abraham nodded and asked, "Will it be OK with the US military, sir?"

"Oh, yes, that's all been sorted out, you will stay here for one week and then be flown back to America."

"But sir, I am a soldier and should go back to France and join my fellow countrymen."

"Listen, Abraham, if you had not come here we may have never been able to expose Doctor Chen's treachery, even though he felt obliged to take orders from the Nazis or his family would die."

Abraham tried to defend Chen and said, "He had no choice really, did he sir?"

"Choice, choice, one must make sacrifices in this life whether in war time or peace."

"Do you mean that you would sacrifice your family in such a dilemma, sir?"

Mr Churchill suddenly went into serious mode and answered, "We are talking about the safety and security of a nation, a nation at war with such evil men that they not only invent, develop and use hideous weapons upon the free world, but they are committing genocide on innocent civilian populations."

Miss Armstrong walked back over and stood next to Abraham, she sensed the tension now developing between the two men and tried to defuse the atmosphere. She remembered something Abraham had told her previously and injected it into the conversation. "Mr Brown has several horses at his farm in Kentucky, sir."

The atmosphere changed immediately, as Abraham and Mr Churchill talked and discussed their love of horses. An hour passed and Mr Churchill noticed the time. "Oh!" he exclaimed. "I must be going."

The room was now nearly empty as most people had gone back to their normal daily duties.

The two men shook hands once more and said goodbye to one another.

As Mr Churchill was escorted out of the room he suddenly stopped and turned back to where Abraham and Miss Armstrong stood. "Remember, young man," he said, "we are a small island nation, and if necessary we have to make sacrifices, whatever the cost to ourselves."

Abraham nodded in approval, for now he understood the decisions that had to be made by the great man and every individual involved in the war effort.

Chapter Forty-Two

As the days passed, Abraham was involved in many different, even bizarre, experiments and tests assessing his abilities and powers. One test proved most useful and would be used by the Allies on several occasions until the end of the war. This came about after Abraham was led into a long wide corridor which was the main linking point for all the different sub-departments of Department S.P.

One hundred people were lined up, and with no knowledge of what was happening, Abraham was asked to walk along the line of men and women. Each person had a number attached to them numbering from one to a hundred. Abraham was given a clip-board, paper and pen and asked to write down any person who made his shoulder ache or hurt. This test had outstanding results, for by way of control, out of the one hundred people in the line, there were five known Nazis who were usually in detention and awaiting trial. As Abraham walked the line he wrote down five numbers as he passed along, these were five, seven, twenty-eight, fifty-one and eighty-nine. All the people with the corresponding numbers attached to them were known Nazis. The test proved to Department S.P. that now if the authorities either in the UK or USA had any suspects who were thought to be Nazis, Abraham would be able to sniff them out with his unusual talent, a talent that a bayonet had been the catalyst for as he faced certain death that day in southern France.

* * * * * *

The week continued, and soon it would be time for Abraham to return to his homeland.

As the weekend approached, Abraham began to feel very uncomfortable, so he told Miss Armstrong about a dream he'd had the previous night. He couldn't predict the future, but he knew something terrible was about to befall the people of London that day. The date was the eighth of September, 1944. In his dream, Abraham had seen a tall, pointed weapon being prepared for an attack on London. His shoulder really hurt now, and he made Miss Armstrong report this to every department and agency, putting them on full alert for something unexpected to happen. People were asking: "What, what is going to happen?" It was just past six in the evening, and as everyone was on alert and very uncertain about the whole thing, already the first V2 rocket was on its trajectory towards London. How could anyone ever envisage such a weapon, fired into outer space and then falling on its flight path to kill civilians with no warning at all; no air raid sirens, no advance warning.

Now London was hit once more by the venomous sting of Mr Hitler's weapon from hell.

As the shock and reality of such an attack became apparent the facts were to be kept secret, as the military and civilian authorities knew that incredible fear and unrest would result if the truth were known, so the attacks were smoke-screened and the destruction blamed on gas explosions.

* * * * * *

The next day, as Abraham was eating his breakfast, Miss Armstrong came into the dining room and sat next to him. They talked briefly about the V2 attacks; she then told him she would be travelling to Devon that day by train, and would like him to join her as she had a surprise for him.

"Sure thing," came his reply, anything to get out of this place. Abraham didn't like being stuck underground all week and confined, he was a farmer and had spent his whole life living and working outdoors, and had become very restless whilst at Department S.P.'s Headquarters.

"You'll be staying overnight in Devon and then we will return here for a de-briefing. After that you'll be flown home the next day."

"Wow, I can't believe it!" he said.

"Meet me back here in twenty minutes, OK?"

"Sure, Miss Armstrong, what's the surprise?" he asked.

"Ah, you will have to wait and see I'm afraid," came her reply.

An hour later they were boarding the train at Waterloo which was heading west to Exeter. They made their way to their seats and were soon ready for the train's departure.

Abraham had never been on a train before and was quite excited by the prospect. The mighty engine that would pull all the carriages now had a full head of steam, and as the guard standing on the platform waved his flag and blew his whistle, the engine driver opened up the valves containing the immense pressure within the large cylinder that stretched from the cab to the front of the train. The train shuddered forward as people leant out from the windows, waving at friends and loved ones. The engine was soon cutting through the air, its large wheels gripping the track as the steam power was transferred to them.

Abraham had never smelt a steam train before and asked Miss Armstrong if he could have a walk around the speeding metal monster.

"Sure, Abraham, I am staying in here if that's all right with you."

Abraham went off to explore the train. People looked at him curiously as it was not usual to see an Afro-American travelling to Devon, and many people admired his smart new uniform which he wore with great pride. As he wandered about the train he came to a railway carriage full of children in each compartment and wondered why, so asked a gentleman having a smoke in the baggage wagon.

"Excuse me, sir, but can you tell me why all those kids are on board this train?"

"What's it to you, fella?" came the reply.

"Oh, nothing sir, but some of them look sad and a few are crying."

"Blame that on the Luftwaffe."

"What do you mean?" asked Abraham.

"You're American, right?"

"Yeah, I've been in London for a week after being injured in southern France."

"Oh, I see, sorry if I was a bit abrupt then. Yes, I'll tell you all about those poor kids."

The man went on to explain to Abraham that these children were evacuees and that they were sent away from London to keep them safe from the bombing raids.

"And where do they go?" enquired Abraham. "I mean, who do they go and stay with?"

"Oh, the poor blighters have to live with families and couples that they have never met before."

"What, you mean total strangers?"

"Yes, that's right fella."

"But that's surely not right."

"Well, it's either that or facing Jerry bombs."

"Is it safer where they end up?" asked Abraham in a concerned manner.

"Oh yes, much safer. They end up in farms and in safe villages well away from the bombings."

Abraham wandered back to his carriage, passing the children once more. He felt great compassion for the people of this island, as even the most innocent of all human life were paying a price for Hitler's madness.

He found their compartment and sat opposite Miss Armstrong. His shoulder tingled and as he looked at her he could not help noticing the heavy frown upon her face. "What's wrong, Miss Armstrong?" he asked.

"Oh, it's just one of my headaches."

"One of your headaches, what do you mean?"

"Every few weeks I get a migraine, I don't know why, and neither do the doctors, so please excuse me if I try and sleep it off for the rest of the journey."

Abraham went into autopilot and asked her to lie down.

"But why?" she enquired.

"Trust me," he said.

Once she was horizontal, Abraham knelt in front of her and placed his right hand on her forehead, and his left hand searched her mid-section for clues. "Please close your eyes and relax," he instructed her.

As she lay there, Abraham remembered the dream he'd had about her the same night he dreamt of Doctor Chen's connection with the Nazis.

In the dream he saw Miss Armstrong as a young girl running through a field, carefree and healthy. The dream sequence kept repeating itself; each time she became a year older. In the last sequence which represented her now, as she ran across the field she slowed down and was inflicted with pain all over.

The field was a wheat field, and as Abraham's dream ended he saw the field enclosed by fences with a sign in each corner, they read 'POISON, KEEP OUT'.

As Abraham placed his hand above her stomach he could feel pain, and knew that her body, now in adult life, was intolerant to wheat; so much so that it was slowly poisoning her in such a way as to inflict crippling headaches and migraines upon her.

Abraham looked at her as she lay there and as he did so, his hands generated a soothing warmth which flowed into Miss Armstrong's body. A crack of static sounded out as a power that could only heal flowed into her, and within a few minutes had dissolved the pain in her head.

She sat up and asked, "How did you do that, Abraham?"

He just smiled and replied, "Oh, it was nothing, nothing at all." He explained to her that her body could no longer accept wheat, and that she would have to find an alternative in life, thus preventing any repetition of further migraines in the future.

Chapter Forty-Three

The journey continued as the train thundered along the tracks, heading west.

"Where are we going, Miss Armstrong?" enquired Abraham.

"Oh, I'm going to visit my parents in Exeter. It's only fifteen miles from where you'll be staying."

"Who will I be staying with?" asked Abraham, who had no idea where he was going.

"Let's just say an old friend is waiting for you and leave it that, shall we?"

Abraham was intrigued but decided to ask no more.

"Are you sure it has been wheat that has given me all those headaches?" asked Miss Armstrong.

"Oh, yes I am one hundred per cent sure."

"Well, that's a bugger for me because I love cakes and bread."

"It's either a life of no wheat or a life of headaches, it's your choice."

Abraham was amazed at the amount of farms and fields that came into view on the journey. The lushness of pasture with cows and sheep grazing, the crops swaying in the breeze basking in the sunshine, and soon the rolling hills of Devon peppered with trees of oak and ash. His thoughts were easy to guess: how nice it would be to live in such a green and pleasant land.

The train entered Devon and was soon slowing down as it approached Axminster. The platform was swarming with people, amongst them some GIs based at Honiton which was the next stop. As the train pulled away, the new passengers filtered into the carriages and compartments, trying to get the few seats that remained free. As Abraham and Miss Armstrong were chatting, three American servicemen made their way towards their compartment. They stood in the doorway and stared at them both. Abraham continued talking to Miss Armstrong but sensed that trouble was lurking. The three men took turns to pretend to cough, thus causing annoyance to Miss Armstrong who turned to face them and said, "Do you want something?"

"Yes," came the reply. "We would like a seat."

"Well, there's four spaces in here so what's the problem? You don't need permission to sit here you know."

"He's the problem."

"What do you mean, he's the problem?"

"He's a Negro and we ain't coming in till he gets up and stands or gets out."

This was the first time since leaving America that Abraham had experienced racism and bigotry. Abraham just sat there and said nothing. Miss Armstrong was now getting a little angry and asked the men to leave.

"Leave? We ain't going nowhere, so the Negro can get out or we will get him out!"

Miss Armstrong was appalled by the racist comments and said, "My friend is not leaving and you are not coming in. OK?"

"Sorry, lady but I am going to count to five and then we are coming in to get him: One – two – three – four – five!"

As the GI reached the fifth count Miss Armstrong stood up. She reached into her bag and pulled out her service revolver. With an icy stare she aimed it at the chief troublemaker and said, "If you step inside or touch him I will touch the trigger. Do I make myself perfectly clear?"

"OK lady, calm down, why are you on his side anyway?"

This remark angered Miss Armstrong even more. She put the gun back into her bag and went and stood face to face with the troublemaker. "I have something for you, something special, are you ready to receive it?" she said.

The GI looked at his two associates and winked. "Yes, please, lady, give it to me."

Miss Armstrong smiled at him. She puckered her lips in a seductive manner and then without any warning, thrust her left knee deeply into his groin.

A moment of silence ensued, followed by the man falling to the floor and curling up in pain, his two comrades recoiling away in disbelief.

Abraham looked on and thought to himself, "Well, he asked for that." He chuckled and squirmed a little at the thought of what the man must be feeling now between his legs. The other GIs helped their comrade to his feet. He looked most embarrassed and made no fuss as the three men went on their way along the train.

"That was pretty harsh, Miss Armstrong," commented Abraham.

"Harsh, no. I did him a favour. Perhaps now he will think twice before using insulting and racist remarks. Sorry you had to witness that but there are times when I don't take shit from anyone."

The train stopped at the next station and off got the three GIs. They waited on the platform until the train set off again. When Abraham and Miss Armstrong's compartment passed them they stared and made rude gestures at the two of them.

"Are you excited Abraham? Because the next stop is where you get off."

The train only travelled a few more miles down the track before stopping at Sidmouth Junction.

Miss Armstrong saw Abraham onto the platform and said, "I will see you back here at midday tomorrow for our return journey to London."

Abraham watched as the train steamed off down the track, Miss Armstrong leaning out of the window and waving goodbye.

Chapter Forty-Four

Abraham stood on the platform and looked around, and as he did so the steam and smoke from the engine blended itself into the light mist that had rolled into the village. People walked down passing him, and once out of the station they dispersed in all directions. Some passengers changed over to the branch line that ran down to Sidmouth.

At the far end of the platform from where he stood, Abraham could see the outline of a man walking steadily towards him. His shoulder warmed and felt good so he started to walk towards the stranger. A dog ran forward to greet Abraham, his tail wagging with excitement. Abraham knelt down to stroke him, he was used to dogs and had two on the farm back in Kentucky. As he was making a fuss of the dog, the stranger came into view. It was Freddie Richards, the pilot he had saved back in France at the monastery.

"I see you have met Charlie."

"Hello, Freddie, so you're the secret person," Abraham replied.

"Yes, and please accept our hospitality by coming and spending the night at our farm."

"And who's this, Freddie?"

"This is Charlie, my springer spaniel, he's a farm dog but I treat him like a pet."

Charlie was an English Springer Spaniel, he was 8 years old and had a beautiful sheen to his coat of black and white fur. Like all dogs, his eyes were alive with energy and playfulness and he was loyal and very loving towards his master.

"Well, Abraham, are you coming?"

"Sure thing," came the reply.

The two men, accompanied by the spaniel, exited the station out to the car park. Freddie walked over to where he had a horse and dray waiting.

"Are we going in that, Freddie?" asked Abraham.

"Oh, yes, come on up. It's only one mile to Fenwater Farm."

The two men set off with the dog happily following them a little way behind. The horse trotted steadily along whilst Abraham took in the new surroundings he now found himself in. They turned right and travelled along a track leading to the farm. The green lush vegetation and peacefulness of the place was the first thing that struck Abraham. As they passed the duck pond and approached the farmhouse he momentarily thought back to the French farmhouse where he had lost his virginity to Emmanuel. "I wonder how she is?" he thought to himself.

Charlie ran on ahead to the front door where Freddie's parents were waiting to greet their American guest. They were called Bob and Jane and had worked the farm after taking it over from Bob's father twenty years earlier.

The horse and dray pulled up in front of the house; Freddie and Abraham alighted and introductions were made.

"Thank you for saving our son's life Abraham," said Bob Richards. "We are indebted to you forever. You are welcome here anytime, now or in the future, so now please think of here as a second home."

Abraham was overwhelmed by the hospitality and sincerity of Mr Richards. He wasn't used to white country folk speaking to him in such a nice way. Back home, many of the neighbouring farm owners were quite rude to coloured people and that was putting it mildly.

"Come on in Abraham. Mum will make us a cup of tea and then I want to show you something special that me and my dad are working on."

Abraham and Bob Richards talked for a while about farming as they slowly drank their tea. Charlie the spaniel curled up in front of Freddie's feet whilst his mother meandered around the house tidying up and finishing off some housework.

"I have never seen a house like this before," said Abraham.

"That's probably because it's over five hundred years old," replied Freddie.

When they had finished drinking their tea and chatting, Bob Richards said he would see them later as he now had to attend to his farm work.

"See you later, Dad," said Freddie. He turned to Abraham and asked, "Are you ready to come and have a look around and then see my little baby?"

Little baby, thought Abraham. *What little baby?*

The two men walked outside where Abraham asked, "What sort of roof do you call that, Freddie?"

"It's called a thatched roof, you will see a lot of them around here."

"Never seen anything like this back home," replied Abraham.

* * * * * *

Freddie showed Abraham all over the main buildings adjoining the farmhouse before heading to a large barn. "Come and see my baby, she's in here."

The two men walked into the barn which contained a large tarpaulin covering something big.

"Give us a hand, Abraham."

The two men pulled the covering back to reveal the fuselage of a Spitfire.

"Well, what do you think of my baby then?" asked Freddie.

"What is it?" said Abraham.

"It's the main body of a Spitfire – the wings are over there under another cover." Freddie went on to explain. "The Spitfire crashed on its return flight back to nearby Exeter Airport. The plane developed a fuel leak after being hit by enemy fire and was only five miles from home when the pilot had to crash land on a neighbouring farm. He was lucky, and OK after the ordeal. Due to the damage it was decided by the Air Force to scrap the Spitfire, so we rescued it and hopefully one day will restore it and maybe get it up into the air again."

Abraham remembered seeing Freddie's Spitfire back in France as he, Patch and Indigo travelled to the monastery. He ran his hands along the fuselage and was amazed by the amount of bullet holes in it.

"Can I get up into the cockpit, Freddie?" he asked.

"Certainly, Abraham, here I'll help you."

Abraham climbed up into the cockpit, and once seated inside could not believe how confined he was.

"There's not a lot of room in here, Freddie. Is this one of the smaller Spitfires?"

Freddie laughed. "No, Abraham, they're all the same size."

As Abraham sat there he realised how brave the pilots were. "You pilots are very brave," he said.

"Well, I never really think about it. You see, we live on this island, a land that I dearly love and will defend with my life if necessary."

"Have you lost many friends and pilots Freddie?" enquired Abraham.

"Yes, I have," replied Freddie as he pictured them in his mind and remembered their individual characters and personalities.

Abraham got down out of the cockpit and stood next to Freddie.

"Come over here, I'll show you the wings, they are pretty smashed up but Dad's sure we can repair them given time."

The two men uncovered the wings as Abraham remembered being struck by the gentle rounded shape of the Spitfire, the first time he had seen one flying. They talked about Spitfires for a while, then Freddie's ear picked up a familiar sound approaching in the distance.

"Come on, Abraham, outside quickly, we may be lucky as it sounds like a couple of Spitfires are coming into Exeter."

They made their way outside and looked up as the planes were nearing. Charlie ran excitedly around his master's legs, the sounds of the engines getting louder and louder as the aircraft approached low overhead. Abraham was once more struck by the beauty and grace of this incredible aerial defender of the island he now stood on.

The two Spitfires touched down a few minutes later at Exeter, one Polish and one British pilot emerged from the aircraft after a successful sortie over northern France. Pilots from many other countries flew Spitfires daily defending British freedom and way of life.

"Would you like to come for a walk with me and Charlie?" asked Freddie.

"Yeah, that sounds a good idea, and please show me around the area if we have time."

The two men set off with the spaniel. They walked through a couple of fields and then followed the River Tale northwards from Fairmile. They passed Escot Church which stood only fifty yards from the river, and carried on for half a mile until they came to a circle of giant redwood trees. Freddie walked up a gently sloping area of grass which looked over the ring of trees and sat down with Abraham. "This is my favourite place in the whole world," said Freddie.

Abraham sensed the peaceful vibration that emanated from the countryside all around him. The two men lay back on the grass whilst Charlie splashed and played in the river below the trees. As they both looked up at the sky, buzzards squawked and high above them the giant birds circled, their eyes watching for any movement from the fields down below.

"I understand why this place is so special to you, Freddie, it does have an incredible feel about it."

In the distance to the north east they could hear the whistle from a steam train as it rolled into Sidmouth Junction. After a while, the two men started to make their way back to Fenwater Farm followed by a now exhausted Charlie who had amused himself for the past hour at the river.

Following their evening meal, Freddie and his parents told Abraham all about the farm and how it had been in their family for at least three hundred years. As Abraham listened to them, he felt a little homesick and thought about how much he loved his mother, sister and brother. As he did so his shoulder tingled lightly and he knew that they were fine.

Chapter Forty-Five

Abraham slept well that night at the farm. The next morning passed quickly and soon it was time to say goodbye to Freddie's parents.

"Thank you for your kind hospitality," said Abraham.

"And thank you once again for saving our son's life. Please come again, you and your family will always be welcome here," said Bob Richards.

Freddie and Abraham set off, the horse and dray taking them back to Sidmouth Junction to meet Miss Armstrong, who would be aboard the midday train back to London Waterloo. Charlie stayed back at the farm as he had work to do that day.

* * * * * *

The two men stood on the platform amongst the other passengers waiting for the train to arrive. As the station clock struck twelve midday, the engine rolled in slowly and stopped. Passengers alighted the train as Abraham looked up and down for his chaperone. There, to the left of him, stood Miss Armstrong.

"Are you ready, Abraham?" she said.

Abraham briefly introduced her to Freddie and then boarded the train with her. The guard walked up through the carriages, letting everyone know that there was a half hour delay. So Abraham and Miss Armstrong stepped off the train and chatted for twenty minutes with Freddie.

Freddie's eyes met Miss Armstrong's several times, and Abraham noted the mutual interest they were now showing towards each other. Freddie could not keep his eyes off Miss Armstrong as the two of them chatted.

"What's your first name, Miss Armstrong?" asked Freddie.

"Why do you want to know?"

"Because I would like to write to you some time if you permit?" replied Freddie.

As she looked at him she had to admit to herself inside that he did look such a dashing young man, with what appeared to be a nice nature about him.

"Trena, my first name is Trena," said Miss Armstrong.

"Here," said Freddie, as he handed her a pencil and scrap of paper. "Write your address down and I will write to you some time."

She jotted down her full name and address in Exeter, and was just handing back the pencil and paper to Freddie when the guard shouted to everyone to get back on to the train.

Abraham and Miss Armstrong once more boarded, the guard's whistle blew and off they went heading eastwards back to London.

Freddie made his way across the road from the station and went into the Railway Hotel which stood opposite Sidmouth Junction. He ordered a pint of ale and sat by a window, reflecting on how lovely Miss Armstrong looked. He put the scrap of paper down in front of him on the table, looking at it now and again as he drank his beer.

* * * * * *

Although the train was running late it made up good time as it journeyed east from Devon. During the journey, Miss Armstrong had asked Abraham lots of questions about Freddie; she seemed most interested in the dashing young man.

When the train finally arrived at Waterloo it was only ten minutes late. They made their way to the station entrance where they were met by a driver from Department S.P. As the jeep made its way through the streets of London, Miss Armstrong opened an envelope given to her by the driver. Her orders were to return with Abraham to Department S.P. where they would stay the night, and then at six o'clock the next morning, Miss Armstrong was to drive him to an airfield where he would board an aeroplane and be flown directly back to America. As she explained her orders to Abraham, his heart and soul warmed at the thought of seeing his family once more. He looked up at the London skyline filled with a sea of barrage balloons, and wondered how Indigo Templeton was doing, was he still alive even? He asked, "What will I be doing on my return home, Miss Armstrong?"

"I think you will be working for your country's own military intelligence, but I guess you will have to wait and see, as neither I nor anyone else at Department S.P. know your own government's military intentions."

* * * * * *

Abraham slept deeply that night and had many dreams, including one of him riding the finest horse he had ever laid eyes on. He also dreamt of Patch Hancock, now at peace with his father. Just as his dreams were coming to an end he saw his own father, who appeared to him and said how proud he was of Abraham.

* * * * * *

It was six in the morning when both Abraham and Miss Armstrong set out from Greenwich to an airfield an hour's drive away.

"This time tomorrow you will be sound asleep in America," said Miss Armstrong.

"Yes, and I hope that I will be allowed to visit my family first," replied Abraham.

"Oh, I'm sure you will."

They drove through the quiet early morning streets of London. It was just getting light and another day was dawning. How many men, women and children would suffer this day in that darkest hour of humanity's history? It was within five miles of the airfield when Abraham and Miss Armstrong both looked up into the clear morning sky to witness the flying formations of many bombers returning home after night time bombing raids on Germany. Abraham felt relief for his homeland as it would never be bombed like London or many of the other British towns and cities.

The jeep made its way to the airfield entrance where it stopped at a checkpoint; two soldiers stood guard and asked for identification and papers. They were allowed through the checkpoint a few minutes later and asked to drive following the road to the right and go to Area 25 where they would be met.

The airfield looked deserted and neither of them could see any aircraft about. As they followed the signs for Area 25 they drove between two rows of nissen huts and then by some almost derelict looking buildings. The road swung left, and as they turned to face the main runway they both looked on in amazement and saw the biggest aeroplane they had ever laid eyes on.

"Am I going home in that?" asked Abraham.

"Looks like it to me, Abraham."

They drove over to a small group of people who were waiting near the aircraft, pulled alongside and turned off the engine. A man stepped forward and introduced himself. He explained a few things to Abraham and then said it was time to board the plane.

Abraham stood and looked at Miss Armstrong. "Goodbye," he said as he embraced her.

"Bye, Abraham, I hope we meet again one day."

"So do I, sweet lady, so do I."

Abraham made his way towards the boarding steps. As he did so he turned back and said, "Don't forget, will you?"

"Forget what, Abraham?"

"No wheat for you or your headaches will always be with you."

"No, I won't forget," she said, waving to Abraham as he boarded the giant plane.

A few other people boarded and the engines roared into life. The plane taxied to the far end of the runway where it turned and launched itself into the wind. As it travelled faster and faster the four gigantic engines pulled it along as their propeller blades cut into the air, the wing flaps now being skilfully positioned by the pilot to give the silver bird lift.

Up, up she went, flying to another continent, across an ocean that spanned two great nations, both speaking a common tongue and both believers in and lovers of freedom and democracy.

Chapter Forty-Six

On the long journey across the Atlantic, Abraham was told that he would be able to spend a few days at home with his family. After that, he would assigned to a Military Intelligence Unit where he would be identifying Nazis, and by using his dreams, trying to stop German military advancements. Several people came and sat with him on the flight, all asking him many different questions.

The plane was only half full in the seating area, the passengers being a mixture of military, scientific and civilian. There was also a very annoying war correspondent amongst them who was continually asking questions. He was very curious as to why Abraham had so many people talking with him so he decided to introduce himself. "Hello, my name is Phillips, and you are…?"

"Abraham, Abraham Brown."

"Abraham Brown, now where have I heard that name before?" The correspondent wandered off, repeating Abraham's name and scratching his head.

* * * * * *

The plane reached mid-Atlantic and Abraham was thinking about everything that had happened to him. He felt so lucky as soon he could hug his mother, brother and sister. He noticed several magazines and newspapers contained in a pocket on the rear of the seat in front of him; he reached forward and started looking through them. Amongst them was a booklet prepared by the US War Department. It was issued to American service personnel sent over to the UK and gave instructions to American servicemen in Britain. Abraham read one particular paragraph and as he did so he thought of British women just like Miss Armstrong – it read:

'British women officers often give orders to men. The men obey smartly and know it is no shame, for British women have proved themselves in this war. They have stuck to their posts near burning ammunition dumps, delivered messages afoot after their motorcycles have been blasted from under them, they have pulled aviators from burning planes, they have died at their gun-posts and as they fell another girl has stepped directly into the position and carried on. There isn't a single record of any British woman in uniform service quitting her post or failing in her duty under fire. Now you understand why British soldiers respect the women in uniform, they have won the right to the utmost respect. When you see a girl in uniform with a bit of ribbon in her tunic remember, she didn't get it for knitting more socks than anyone else in Ipswich'

(GI Handbook 1942).

* * * * * *

The war correspondent returned, "Abraham Brown, you're the guy who saved the Americans at that bridge."

Abraham just nodded and smiled at him.

"Can I take a few photos please, Mr Brown."

After a while, Abraham agreed to a couple of photos being taken and a few minutes of questions from Phillips.

Abraham knew that if he didn't agree he would probably be pestered for the many more remaining hours during the flight.

* * * * * *

The large silver bird landed back on American soil.

Abraham was transferred to a smaller plane and flown to Kentucky. During the flight he looked down at the landscape that he was used to and thanked God in his heart for his safe return home.

The aircraft touched down forty miles from the farm. A car was waiting for him and soon he was on the last stage of the long journey home.

A mile from the farm, Abraham asked the driver to stop; the driver looked puzzled by this request.

"Just let me out here please."

"OK mister, if that's what you want," and with that the car turned round and headed back the way it had come.

Abraham carried a small bag with him as he set out on foot. As he walked he felt the air in his lungs; the beat of his heart became excited, as soon he would be home. The sun bathed him with a warm welcome as his feet trod the ground of his birthplace. The crops swayed at him, moved by an invisible current of air.

As he walked, he started to whistle the tune that his father had taught him. He turned the corner and faced the driveway of the house and three pairs of ears inside heard and recognised the whistle, and with that his family charged outside to see.

Abraham dropped his bag as he set eyes upon his mother, brother and sister standing in front of the house. They ran towards each other and embraced, the tears of joy sprinkling upon the ground.

* * * * * *

That evening, around the tea table, Abraham told his family of his time in Europe and they listened attentively as he spoke.

"Your father would be so proud of you Abraham," said Mrs Brown. "We are all so proud of you son. You look tired. Why don't you get on to bed and tomorrow we shall all start the day as a family once more."

"OK Ma, I will." Abraham said goodnight and retired to his room until morning.

That night, for the first time since being skewered by a bayonet, Abraham did not dream.

Chapter Forty-Seven

The next day Abraham awoke and went to the kitchen where everyone was at breakfast, his mother's cooking making him feel even more at home, the smells and tastes he knew so well.

They had just finished eating when a car drove up to the house and out clambered Mr Henderson, the landowner, who walked slowly up to the house. He was overweight and wore a white shirt. His trousers were held up with braces and he always carried a cotton cloth to mop his brow as his almost bald head was nearly always sweating.

Abraham and his mother stepped outside to see who it was.

"Oh dear, Abraham, there is something I have not told you."

"What, Ma? Please tell me."

"We couldn't pay all the rent for last month and I fear what Mr Henderson has now come to tell us."

As Abraham looked at the approaching figure of Mr Henderson, he couldn't help comparing his facial features and round head with that of Mr Churchill who had thanked him at Department S.P. back in London. They walked down the steps to meet him.

"Please Mr Henderson sir, give us a little more time to give you the money we owe," said Mrs Brown.

Abraham's shoulder warmed as he put his arm around his mother.

"Back from the war are we, Abraham Brown?" said Mr Henderson in an enquiring voice.

"Just visiting for a few days and then back on active service," replied Abraham.

"I have been thinking about the money you owe me, Mrs Brown and it's not good enough, you know, so shall I tell you what I intend to do?"

Abraham felt a little puzzled by this as his shoulder still warmed and tingled slightly, so he just let Mr Henderson carry on.

Then something totally unexpected happened as Mr Henderson asked, "Can I come into the house and have some coffee?"

This threw Mrs Brown for a moment so Abraham replied, "Yes, you are most welcome."

Abraham and his mother went back into the house followed by Mr Henderson. He wasn't very fit and puffed and panted heavily as he climbed the steps. Once inside, Abraham offered a chair to him as Mrs Brown got him a coffee.

Abraham's siblings George and Eleanor were sent to do their chores on the farm as Abraham and his mother sat and waited to hear what Mr Henderson had decided. He finished his coffee and looked up at Abraham, his whole face now looking different than ever before. "I know about your heroism in southern France, Abraham. I also served our country and was in France during the last war and lost many comrades. You have saved many young Americans and I salute you, Abraham Brown."

Abraham now knew why his shoulder had warmed. His mother sat in a state of shock, as for all the years she had known him, she had thought that Mr Henderson was a hard-nosed bastard.

"Abraham, I hold my head in shame and ask one thing of you and your family."

Abraham now instinctively trusted the man who now appeared to be more human than anyone had ever known him. "Please go on," said Abraham.

"Forget the money you owe me."

Mrs Brown let out a gasp of surprise.

"From today, I am going to halve your rent."

Now Abraham let out a gasp.

"Please accept a gift."

"A gift?" said Mrs Brown.

"Yes, a gift. The field behind this farmhouse I now give to you and will get the deeds signed over to you as soon as I can. All my life I have been greedy and really have nothing to show for it, whereas you, Abraham, are a hero, and a better American than I have ever been."

As Mr Henderson drove away, Mrs Brown turned to Abraham and said, "Son, you have returned safely and now, God willing, we can make a small profit each year on the farm."

"Yes Ma, we will. I have to report back in a few days but will be based here on American soil for the rest of the war."

* * * * * *

The days passed quickly and the following week, Abraham was at his new post in Military Intelligence. During the remainder of the war, he successfully identified several more suspected Nazis and was decorated for his heroism in France.

* * * * * *

Back at the farm in Kentucky, people would come and pose for photos in front of Abraham's home.

The war correspondent, Phillips, who Abraham had met on the plane back from Europe had put together a large article which was printed in many newspapers across the United States.

* * * * * *

By the end of 1945 both the Germans and the Japanese had surrendered.

Those brave Allied troops had saved the world from their savage tyranny.

* * * * * *

To those who gave their lives for us

May heaven embrace their souls and hold them in high esteem as heroes of the free world

Never to be forgotten

Amen

Epilogue

July 4th 1945

Abraham is on leave and is mending some fencing along the roadside when a large vehicle rolls up. The driver says he has a delivery for a Mr Abraham Brown. To his surprise the most beautiful horse he had ever seen is led out of the back of the truck. Abraham is handed an envelope. Inside it reads 'To Abraham Brown, with thanks and gratitude from the British nation'. The letter is signed, Winston Churchill.

* * * * * *

April 7th 1946

The bridge that was destroyed by the Germans has now been repaired and re-opened. It is named Hancock's Bridge in memory of Patch Hancock.

* * * * * *

September 1st 1947

After two years of courtship, Freddie Richards marries Miss Trena Armstrong. The wedding ceremony is held at Escot Church, Fairmile, Devon.

* * * * * *

June 5th 1948

After a short romance, Abraham marries Miss Martha Strong. The wedding guests include Indigo Templeton and the landowner Mr Henderson who manages to eat more than anyone else.

* * * * * *

May 8th 1949

Freddie Richards and his father have finished repairing and renovating the Spitfire. On this day he flies to France and over the monastery where the brothers from the Order of the Tree of Life wave to him. He then flies over Hancock's Bridge, doing a victory roll, before re-fuelling and returning to Devon.

* * * * * *

March 11th 1950

A new town is emerging, built a few miles from Abraham's farm. To everyone's delight it is named after Abraham and is called Brownstown.

* * * * * *

November 12th 1951

Indigo Templeton passes his Doctor's exam and becomes a registered Medical Doctor.

Sickened by the violence of war, he decides to devote his life to helping others.

* * * * * *

June 5th 1975 – Brownstown twelve noon

Abraham is walking home after getting his hair cut. He carries a newspaper in his hand and lightly taps it against walls and fences as he walks the last block.

"Afternoon, Abraham," says a woman in her garden.

He tips his hat to her and smiles. As he travels the last hundred yards to his house, he sees a figure sitting on his front step. Some kids cycle by and stop, one of them saying to him, "Hey, Mr Brown, who's that lady sat on your step, she sure is pretty."

Abraham's step quickens as his curiosity increases, his shoulder warms, tingles and feels like never before. His neighbours have noticed the woman waiting for him; several of them stand outside their houses waiting to see what's going on. Abraham notices she has a suitcase by her side and now walks quickly up the pathway to the house. She stands up and they face one another, their own minds asking questions about each other.

* * * * * *

It is exactly one year ago from today that Abraham's wife, Martha, died after being struck by a car whilst crossing a busy street.

They never had any children together, which was something that saddened them both over the years.

Since Martha's death, every night Abraham has dreamt of a woman calling out to him. She reaches out to touch him and then the dream ends.

Now, three hundred and sixty-five days later, she is standing facing him, her hair Afro styled. She wears an orange catsuit and Abraham marvels at her beauty. He is almost mesmerised and cannot work out who she is or why she has been in his dreams.

"Can I help you, young lady?" he asks.

"I am looking for Abraham Brown," she replies.

"That is my name, but I am sure there are many men in these parts with the same name. How do you know it is me you are seeking?" Abraham notices that she has a foreign accent which he instantly recognises as French.

"My name is Nicole, and I am looking for the owner of these." She reaches into her bag and withdraws her hand which is closed, her fingers tightly wrapped around something.

Abraham looks intensely at her hand as she holds it in front of him and slowly opens it.

There, in the palm of her hand, lies a set of dog tags.

Abraham looks in disbelief and then reaches out for them, his shoulder now electrified in reaction to this occurrence. "Where did you get these, young lady?"

"Call me by my name please."

"OK, where did you find these, please, Nicole?"

"Can we go inside please Mr Brown? I have something important to tell you."

"Oh, I am sorry, please come in, let me take your bag."

Abraham leads her into the house where his Jack Russell patiently awaits him. He leads the dog out to the back yard and then returns inside. He sits down opposite Nicole, his hands exploring the dog tags as he wonders to himself where she had found them.

The large clock on the wall ticks away and the rays of sunlight flicker into the room through the window, as a light wind blows the branches on the tree outside, giving shade to the front of the house.

"Now young lady, tell me about these dog tags."

"My mother gave them to me."

"Your mother?" says Abraham in surprise.

"Yes, my mother. You see she died exactly one year ago today."

Abraham is thinking of Martha, and that this is such a strange coincidence.

"Why did she have them?" enquires Abraham.

"Throughout her life she would never tell me who my father was. All she would say when I asked about him was that he was the most beautiful man she had ever met."

"So why have you come here today Nicole?"

"The day before she died she asked me to get her a small box from the cupboard which contained these dog tags. I gave them to her, she kissed them and then placed them in my hands. My mother, Emmanuel, told me that the dog tags belonged to my father and that there could be a chance of me finding him."

* * * * * *

Abraham now knew this was his daughter. Nicole now knew she had found her father.

They talked for a long time, Abraham explaining that he had no knowledge about her being born.

She knew and understood this, and soon they both felt as though the missing jigsaw piece of their lives had now been found.

Abraham went to the kitchen to make them both coffee, and as he did so he let the Jack Russell back into the house.

The dog ran straight to Nicole and started to lick her face and play with her.

The Jack Russell had a large dark area of fur on his head and surrounding one eye.

"What do you call your dog?" asked Nicole.

"Oh, I call him Patch – PATCH HANCOCK."

THE END